FLOORS

From the Chicken House

I still get a lift when I visit hotels (even when I have to take the stairs)! I love reading the little booklets and trying out all the switches, and imagining whether the stray small staircases lead to mysterious extra rooms! But I've never stayed anywhere as *extraordinary* and *exciting* as the Whippet.

Patrick Carman has hidden cunning surprises on every floor of his hotel, alongside some unexpected wildlife (although, come to think of it, one hotel did give me a rubber duck once).

There are some places you never want to leave and this hotel is sure to be one to add to your favourites list of chocolate factories and wizard schools.

Barry Cunningham
Publisher

FLOORS

PATRICK CARMAN

Chicken
House

2 Palmer Street, Frome, Somerset BA11 1DS

Text © 2011 by Patrick Carman.

Published by arrangement with Scholastic Inc., 557 Broadway, New York 10012,
USA
The proprietor hereby maintains that the Author asserts his moral rights to be
identified as the Proprietor of the Work.

First published by Scholastic Inc., 557 Broadway, New York 10012, USA in 2011

First published in Great Britain in 2012
The Chicken House
2 Palmer Street
Frome, Somerset BA11 1DS
United Kingdom
www.doublecluck.com

Patrick Carman has asserted his rights under the Copyright, Designs and Patents Act,
1988, to be identified as the author of this work.

Cover illustration by David Wyatt
Cover design by Steve Wells
Illustrations by Chris Turnham
Typeset by Dorchester Typesetting Group Ltd
Printed and bound in Great Britain by CPI Group (UK) Ltd, Croydon, CR0 4YY

The paper used in this Chicken House book is made from wood
grown in sustainable forests.

1 3 5 7 9 10 8 6 4 2

British Library Cataloguing in Publication data available.

ISBN 978-1-906427-90-0

For Riley, whose imagination inspires me

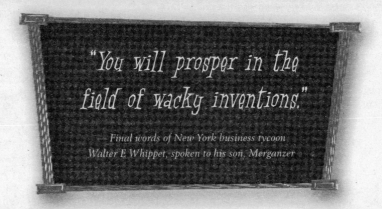

Merganzer Whippet was an impulsive young man of fifteen when he raced into his father's room just in time to hear these fateful words. Merganzer had just finished his tenth consecutive year of boarding school, during which his father had been busy building a financial empire. Needless to say, the two had never been close.

The words were not the sort of thing Merganzer's father was known for saying. People close to the old man would have expected something like *Buy cheap, sell high! And whatever you do, don't squander the family fortune.* But twelve seconds later, Walter E Whippet was dead. *You will prosper in the field of wacky inventions* were the only words of advice Merganzer had been given.

If only Merganzer had known they were spoken by a man who'd been talking gibberish for weeks.

Things might have turned out differently.

CHAPTER 1

TO THE ROOF!

Leo Fillmore awoke to the sound of snipping. It was Mr Phipps, the gardener, trimming and shaping the bushes outside the small window, his ghostly shadow moving across the basement walls. Every Monday at the crack of dawn, Mr Phipps trimmed outside Leo's window, the echo of the shears like a voice that seemed to say *Wake up, wake up, wake up!*

Leo sat up in bed and thought first of his mother's voice; then he thought of ducks and breakfast. After that, he remembered the one thing he'd hoped to forget in his sleep: Merganzer D Whippet, the owner and creator of the Whippet Hotel, was gone. He'd been gone a long time – one hundred days and counting – and Leo was beginning to wonder if the man who'd built the most extraordinary hotel in the world would ever find his way back. He tried to set this thought aside as he watched Mr Phipps's shadow pass by.

Leo was a small boy of ten, with a sizeable blob of curly hair on top of his head. Were she still alive, his mother would have cut it months ago. Sometimes Mr Phipps, who was quiet by nature, would look at Leo's head as if it were a tall green hedge that needed trimming.

When Leo's mother died, he and his father had moved into the basement boiler room from which the two of them took care of the Whippet Hotel. Five years later, it felt like the only home Leo knew. They slept on camp beds separated by a glugging Whirlpool washing machine. There was a desk made of breeze blocks with an old door for a top, piled high with tools and manuals and receipts. The basement window let in soft light and shadows. There were other, larger tools and boxes everywhere, and shelves full of old doorknobs and hotel parts. In the dampest, darkest corner of the basement sat a giant, leaking boiler.

It may sound as if the basement of the Whippet

Hotel was a shabby sort of place to live, but it was cosy and especially cool in the hot summer months. Leo loved the warm sounds and smells, his thread-bare blanket, the tiny kitchen that folded down from one of the walls and the gulping boiler that never seemed to sleep.

As Mr Phipps moved on, the sound of snipping growing softer outside the window, Leo tiptoed to the coffee maker and the paint-splattered sink. Soon enough, the coffee pot filled the basement with the rich smell of morning, and Leo's father started to stir. A few minutes later, Clarence and Leo Fillmore stood in their pyjamas before the call centre, taking stock of the day that lay ahead. The call centre occupied all the space above the makeshift desk, and it was but one example of the strange and unusual things Mr Whippet had created throughout the hotel. There were bells and buzzers and lights on the wall that flashed and spun. There was a horn with brass pipes that twisted all along the ceiling. There were dials, banks of buttons and meters with water pressure readings and temperatures. And in the very centre of it all was a shark's head, its crooked teeth smiling gleefully. Under the shark's head was the word *Daisy*, presumably the shark's name. Daisy looked as if she had come blasting through the wall and got stuck there, for ever cursed to deliver messages in the Whippet Hotel basement.

"We've got about thirty seconds before she wakes up," said Clarence Fillmore, slurping his coffee and scratching the grey stubble on his chin. Daisy's eyes were closed as if she were in a dream, chasing a school of terrified goldfish. "We'd better get out of these pyjamas."

Leo knew better than to doubt his dad's intuition. Clarence Fillmore had an uncanny sense of timing when it came to the Whippet Hotel and its many needs, so Leo had already pulled on his maintenance overalls by the time the first message arrived.

Daisy's eyes opened wide and the sound of a ticker-tape machine filled the basement. Lights blinked yellow and green, a sign that whatever message Daisy was about to deliver was not a catastrophe. If a water main had burst or the air con-ditioning had gone on the blink, there would have been a siren wail and red lights, which were both very unpleasant at the crack of dawn.

A thin strip of white paper, like an endless receipt out of a supermarket till, curled out of Daisy's mouth.

"Ms Sparks, as I suspected," Clarence said, ripping

the curling paper from the shark's crooked teeth with his big hand. "It wouldn't be Monday morning at the Whippet without her."

Leo took one end of the long, curled strip of paper in his hand and looked at it curiously. "I used to think Mr Whippet was in charge of the orders, even if they came from someone else," he said. "I guess I was wrong."

Clarence Fillmore looked at his son and felt a little sad for the boy.

"You know Mr Whippet wouldn't leave for good without the ducks," Clarence said. "Stay focused, Leo. It will take your mind off your troubles. And besides, the last thing we need is Ms Sparks breathing down our necks all day."

Clarence Fillmore was a big, lumbering man, often slow to speak. Like a giant in the basement, he was constantly ducking under pipes and ductwork. Leo had long understood that these characteristics of his father's made some people think Clarence was a simple maintenance man without much going on upstairs. Nothing could have been further from the truth. Taking care of a hotel, especially *this* hotel, required an encyclopedic understanding of architecture, machinery, cooling systems, heating systems, plumbing, duck control and a million other things. Without his dad on the job, Leo suspected, the Whippet Hotel would probably keel over within a week.

"A day without Ms Sparks would be nice," Leo said. "Sometimes I wish she'd go on holiday and never come back."

Ms Sparks, who had become more and more demanding each day Mr Whippet did not return, was the desk clerk and general manager of the hotel. She had long fingers for pointing out all the things Leo and his father hadn't done, and she wore an outrageous beehive hairdo that seemed to say *I am in charge here. Don't cross me*. Whenever Ms Sparks gave a command to the maid or the gardener or anyone else, she leaned forwards and gave them the evil eye, her great head of hair teetering over whomever she was ordering around, casting a dark shadow.

On this particular day, Ms Sparks's ticker-tape list of things to do was over a metre long. Before Mr Fillmore could read the entire thing, Daisy was at it again, only this time the paper was pink and the red siren was spinning and howling in the basement.

Leo tore the ticker tape from the shark's mouth and Mr Fillmore flipped a switch on the call centre, silencing the alarm.

Leo read the pink message: *The ducks are on the ledge!!*

Leo stared at his father, hoping against all hope he would be sent to the roof of the Whippet Hotel.

"Did she use an exclamation mark?" Clarence asked, sipping once again at his coffee and rubbing his temple.

"Two of them," Leo replied, handing over the pink ticker tape. His dad examined the note carefully.

"The last thing we need is Betty wandering around the hotel, biting the guests. The sooner you get up there, the better."

Leo grabbed one of the hotel walkie-talkies and headed for the door before his dad could change his mind.

"Hold on a second," said Mr Fillmore, and Leo thought for sure he would be told to work in the maintenance tunnel instead. He could already hear the order to fix the pipes on the third floor instead of walking the ducks.

But Mr Fillmore had something else in mind, something he hoped would raise his son's spirits, if only a little. He stared at a panel of coloured knobs and pressed a red one with the meaty palm of his hand. Then he typed some letters on a keypad and a key card began to emerge from the call-centre wall. Words were being etched on to the card as it came out, but Leo couldn't see what they were.

"This should do the trick," Mr Fillmore said, handing Leo the key card. "Just be careful. And buckle up this time. We don't want any more bloody noses so early in the week. You know how Ms Sparks overreacts."

Leo had held many Whippet Hotel key cards, which were about the size and shape of a credit card. But each Whippet Hotel key card was special. For starters, no one but Merganzer D Whippet knew how they were made or what they did. It was rumoured they tracked the recipient's every move, monitored vital signs, even read minds. If you had a long-stay room at the Whippet, you had a yellow key card. A short-stay card was green.

Clarence Fillmore and Ms Sparks had blue key cards, which opened many doors. And then there were the red Whippet cards, like the one Leo held in his hand. These were one-time-use key cards. Once they were inserted into a wall or a door, they vanished.

There was one other card – the silver key card – that Mr Whippet kept in his pocket on a matching silver chain. This card opened every single room in the hotel . . . even the secret rooms that almost no one had ever seen.

The edges of Leo's red key card were lined with wispy shapes and lines, and in the centre were the words *To the Roof, Pronto!* No finer words had ever been printed on a Monday morning.

"The Double Helix?" Leo whispered, excitement welling up in his voice.

"You know what *Pronto!* means – now get going before I change my mind," said Mr Fillmore.

A few seconds later, Leo was running up the basement stairs into the lobby of the Whippet Hotel, thinking what a perfect Monday morning it was turning out to be.

Usually, when it was time to walk the ducks, Leo used the duck elevator to make the long climb up to the roof. The duck elevator was a contraption very much like an ordinary elevator, only shorter, narrower, slower and bursting with the aroma of wet feathers. But this was an emergency – time was of the essence – and that meant he'd have to use a different, more secret way to the top of the Whippet Hotel.

Leo stood before Ms Sparks and felt the shadow

of her beehive hairdo as he held out the Whippet key.

"It's a *Pronto!* key card," Leo explained. "See, it says so, right there."

Ms Sparks's pencil-thin eyebrows went up as she lurched forwards over her desk, reading glasses dangling precariously on the very tip of her nose. Then, as was her custom, she delicately pinched the Whippet key card and tugged it out of the boy's hand. She scratched the card with a fingernail to test its authenticity.

Once the key card had passed inspection, Ms Sparks chided, "If Betty bites another guest, I'm blaming you."

Betty was the head duck, a real troublemaker when she wanted to be, but Leo knew how to keep her calm and happy. Ms Sparks hated ducks – Betty in particular – and she loathed the maintenance crew, otherwise known as Leo and Clarence Fillmore.

"Don't worry about Betty," Leo said. "I can handle her. I brought treats."

Leo patted the front pocket of his overalls just to be sure he had what he needed. While he did, the new summer bellboy began creeping ever so slowly away from the front door towards them. His mum was Pilar, the hotel maid. She'd been with the

Whippet a long time, but this was the first summer her son had been allowed to work at the hotel.

The boy arrived at Leo's shoulder, staring down at the key card.

"You have a *Pronto!* card," said the boy. "Lucky you."

Leo nodded and tried not to smile with too much excitement at the shorter, darker-skinned kid in the smart red uniform. How did he even know about *Pronto!* cards?

"Remi, door, now!" barked Ms Sparks, and the new boy hurried back to his post, where he stood staring morosely at the floor, glancing up now and again to see what was about to happen. Leo felt sorry for him, stuck as he was in the lobby with Ms Sparks all day. The poor guy must be cursed.

Ms Sparks turned to a bright green statue of a frog on her desk. It had a big belly, like a frog Buddha, and it was laughing. She placed the card in a slot right about where the frog's belly button would be if it had one, and the card disappeared. This sent two orange marbles shooting out of the frog's head towards the ceiling, landing perfectly on two metal tracks that twisted and turned wildly overhead. Watching the marbles make their way down the tracks gave Leo a chance to take in the entire lobby. The space was dominated by huge green plants carved into the shapes of animals, set against purple walls. There was an elevator with polished gold doors – strictly for guests – and a wide, ornate staircase with a red carpet and dark wood banisters.

The orange marbles followed the tracks to a green giraffe, twisting around its neck until they hit a long straight section and disappeared into two holes above a little orange door. The door creaked open ever so slightly and Ms Sparks leaned over the desk, once more giving Leo a look of death. The new bellboy stole a longing glance at the orange door, but didn't have the courage to come closer.

"Do NOT, under any circumstances, put a duck in there," Ms Sparks commanded sternly. "If you have a duck on your person, use the duck elevator."

"Yes, ma'am," said Leo. "No ducks where ducks don't belong. I wouldn't think of it."

Captain Rickenbacker, who had shown up two years ago and hadn't left the building since, entered the lobby with his red cape flapping behind him. He was a technology millionaire many times over, but he'd grown weary of the stress and the computer screens. Ms Sparks liked to say he'd gone a little off his rocker, but Leo wasn't so sure. Captain Rickenbacker had fallen head over heels for the hotel from the moment he'd set foot in the lobby. He loved the Whippet Hotel. It made him happy. It made him content. And so he had stayed – two years running – on the third floor, in one of the oddest rooms in the hotel.

Leo knew better than to get into a conversation with Captain Rickenbacker – it could take a long time – so he quickly opened the small orange door and went inside. He looked back at the bellboy, who gave him a thumbs-up. Leo returned the gesture and closed the orange door behind him.

Once the door was shut, Leo knew what to do. He'd been inside several times before, always with Mr Whippet. Being alone now made him miss Merganzer Whippet even more.

Leo put these thoughts aside and walked the few short steps in the near darkness to a seat next to a set of twisting poles that seemed to rise endlessly into the dark above. Sitting on the seat made the poles glow dimly – one orange, the other red – and suddenly the tunnel leading up was full of white dots, like stars in the sky.

This is going to be good, Leo thought, first buckling

himself in with the seat belt, then pulling the shoulder bar down. It felt like being on a roller coaster, only better, because Leo knew what came next. No sooner was he strapped in than the Double Helix, which is what Mr Whippet called it, sent Leo twisting up the centre of the Whippet Hotel like a wound-up bolt of lightning. His face felt as if it was melting as the Double Helix flew up and up, rounding the glowing poles as it went, arriving at the roof in five seconds flat. Stopping was almost as fun as taking off, and it was the main reason wearing the seat belt was a good idea.

I don't think I'll ever get tired of that, even when I'm a hundred years old, Leo thought. He'd arrived on the roof right next to the pond, from where three ducks observed him curiously. They all had the same iridescent green heads, bright orange beaks and black and white feathers.

"Step away from the ledge, Betty," Leo said as he got out of the Double Helix and walked slowly towards the other side of the pond. The roof was open-air, and Betty, the largest duck of the six and the only one with all black feathers, had convinced two other ducks to join her on the ledge.

"I have treats," said Leo, digging into his front

pocket and pulling out three slices of pumpernickel bread. Betty was off the ledge in a flash, followed by the other two, and then by three more swimming out of the pond.

Now Leo was surrounded by all six ducks, each of them quacking for some pumpernickel.

"What you really need is a good long walk in the grounds," said Leo, tearing off bits of dark bread as he inched his way towards the duck elevator. Betty and the other ducks were like dogs, really – if they had a good long walk every day and they got fed, they were happy on the roof. But if they were left alone for too long, they grew restless and irritable. They'd fly down to the lobby and start biting people.

Leo threw open the wooden door to the duck elevator and a puff of feathers filled the air. He turned to watch the line of ducks follow after Betty as they crowded inside, filling nearly the entire space before Leo could cram himself inside and shut the door, trapped with six noisy quackers. He pulled the DOWN lever, knowing it would be a long, slow journey to the lobby, nothing like the Double Helix. But soon enough, he'd be walking the ducks, something he and Merganzer D Whippet had done together before the maker of the hotel had vanished so unexpectedly.

Leo sighed deeply and stared at his feet. There wasn't much light in the duck elevator, and it felt even more cramped than usual.

"You guys are eating too much pumpernickel. I can barely fit in here any more."

He would have done well to pay closer attention to the inside of the little elevator, for something new was hidden inside.

Leo's life was about to change for ever.

―――――――――――

On the fifteenth floor of a New York hotel, two men stared out of a window. One wore an expensive-looking grey fedora with a soft black band around the middle. In fact, everything Bernard Frescobaldi wore looked expensive: a three-piece suit, shiny cufflinks, a silky gold tie – appropriate attire for an Italian land baron on the hunt for a bargain.

"Let me see our most recent report once more," Bernard demanded, squinting through a pair of high-powered binoculars, trying with all his might to get a better look at the Whippet Hotel.

"As you wish, sir."

Bernard Frescobaldi's assistant, Milton, clicked open a silver metal briefcase and removed a manila envelope marked *Private: Keep out!*

Inside were research documents, surveillance reports, dozens of photographs of the Whippet Hotel and a collection of private papers. Milton removed the top sheet and handed it to Bernard for his inspection.

Bernard reviewed the document before him for the hundredth time.

Field Report, Whippet Hotel – June 21

Upon his untimely death, the billionaire Walter E Whippet left his entire fortune to his son, Merganzer. Years later, Merganzer D Whippet purchased one entire square block, had every building torn down, and spent the next six years building the strangest hotel anyone has ever seen.

From the beginning, deep mystery has shrouded the Whippet. It's a shockingly small hotel on an enormous site in a city known for taking advantage of every square centimetre of space. There are only nine floors, or so it seems from the outside, and each floor has an unknown number of rooms. The roof houses a pond, for Merganzer D Whippet is obsessed with ducks. Rumours abound of countless hidden passageways and secret rooms, known only to a few.

The Whippet's design is alarmingly off-kilter – it

appears to wobble in the slightest gust of wind. Some say a child could spit on the Whippet and it would fall over, though this seems highly unlikely. And then there are the grounds, vast and useless, a colossal waste of space. Giant bushes carved into the shapes of ducks tower over the winding paths that surround the hotel, which only serve to make the Whippet look even smaller than it actually is. Along the pavement runs a tall iron fence with a gate that opens only for deliveries and guests with special yellow or green key cards.

If passers-by on the outside of the Whippet think it's strange, they're in for an even bigger surprise should they ever choose to stay there. Not many people do. The Whippet is outlandishly exclusive and gossip flies all over town about the actual cost of a room and what might be found inside. Wanting to stay is one thing; being able to stay has much more to do with how fabulously wealthy a person is. There are those who say Merganzer planned it this way, because he didn't really want anyone to come round. He's busy tinkering, making things, playing with the ducks and (as you well know by now) disappearing entirely.

It would appear that Merganzer D Whippet has left the city. Chances are he's at the South Pole, honking at the moon.

Bernard went back to staring out of the window, a glimmer in his eye as he handed the report back to Milton.

"It's time we put our plan into action," Bernard announced. He was a tall man, thin but sturdy, and his sharp nose crinkled with excitement.

Milton was shorter, rounder and more excitable. His fingers danced with anticipation as he jingled the keys to the black town car awaiting them downstairs.

"As you wish, sir. As you wish!"

· CHAPTER 2 ·

THE PURPLE BOX

Betty was staring at Leo, her bill only a few centimetres away, quacking softly in his face. Her breath smelled like daffodils.

"You've been eating the flowers in the grounds again, haven't you?" Leo asked. "Mr Phipps will have a fit if he finds out. I've been blaming it on the crows, but now you'll have to come clean."

Betty almost seemed to understand what Leo was saying. She drooped her head and let out what could only be described as a long sigh in the form of a dying quack.

"I'm only kidding. I won't tell."

Betty brightened and moved a step closer, digging

her orange bill into the front pocket of Leo's overalls.

"You're all going on a diet. Look how cramped I am in this little corner!"

Betty glanced at Leo then, and if the boy hadn't known better, he'd have said the duck was scowling at him. No duck likes a diet.

But it was true that the duck elevator felt unusually cramped. The long ride down seemed to last forever, and the ducks were restless, wobbling back and forth on their webbed feet and climbing all over Leo, looking for pumpernickel.

When the duck elevator opened onto the lobby, Leo told Betty to wait, which she did. When Betty waited, they all waited, and this gave Leo time to crawl out and find Merganzer's walking stick. It was formed from one long, gnarled branch, its handle smooth and round. Without it, the ducks wouldn't follow. There seemed to be magic in the walking stick, and after taking it from its cupboard, Leo returned to the duck elevator, stood before the group of them, and moved the walking stick across the floor. The six ducks marched out, Betty at the front.

It wasn't until they were all out of the duck elevator that Leo saw the purple box.

"What's this?" he whispered, barely hearing his

own words. The ducks hadn't grown larger after all; there had simply been less space for them to stand in. Leo leaned inside for a closer look and saw that the purple box was around fifteen centimetres tall and thirty centimetres wide, with a seal on top that could not be mistaken:

"Merganzer!" said Leo, edging into the small space so he could touch the mysterious box.

"Get these ducks out of the lobby this instant!" yelled Ms Sparks. "Move it, move it, move it!"

The ducks were alarmed by her voice, and Leo began to lose control of the situation. The new bellboy, having gathered his courage, was inching his way towards the duck elevator. Leo couldn't let anyone see what he'd found, but Betty had a look on her face that said *I am seconds away from biting someone's ankle*.

Leo slammed the duck elevator door shut with a *POW!* before the purple box could be seen, then pushed the UP lever, sending the contraption on a five-minute journey back to the roof. That was the final straw for Betty and her pals. She flew up to Ms

Sparks's desk and nearly crashed into her beehive hairdo. The rest of the ducks went into hysterics, flapping all over the room like dive-bombers.

"Open the door!" Ms Sparks screamed, waving her arms as if a thousand wild bats were on a crash course with her face. The bellboy bolted back to the lobby entrance and pushed his small frame against the big glass door.

It was mayhem in the lobby when Leo's father arrived from the basement. He looked at Leo, then reached out his hand for the walking stick.

Clarence Fillmore was a towering figure with a calming effect. He whistled three times fast, then tapped the stick on the marble floor and walked out of the door. The ducks flew outside and landed in a birdbath way too small for so many large birds, where they huddled together, waiting for their promised walk through the grounds.

"Remi, feathers, now!" said Ms Sparks, which sent the bellboy tearing around the lobby, picking up all the feathers that had come loose. From this, and Ms Sparks's earlier command, Leo realized the new boy's name had to be Remi, but there was no time for formal introductions as he skirted past and out on to the front steps.

Mr Fillmore got an earful from Ms Sparks about the inadequate skills of his duck-walking son, but Leo didn't seem to mind. All he could think about was the purple box, which was safe, at least for the moment.

What did it mean? Where had it come from? And why did it have Merganzer D Whippet's head emblazoned on its top?

———————————

Leo could think of little else besides the purple box as he walked the long and winding path in the hotel grounds. Betty and the rest of the ducks waddled contentedly behind him in a line, following Merganzer's walking stick to the farthest reaches of the grounds. At the most distant corner was a small pond, where all the ducks went swimming and bobbing for who-knew-what. While they did, Leo sat on a stone bench wishing he could get out of all the work he'd have to do when he returned to the hotel.

"Why so glum?"

Leo jumped at the sound of the slow Texas drawl behind him. It was LillyAnn Pompadore, who'd been staying at the hotel for almost three months. She was fabulously rich, or so Leo had been told, hiding out from a Texas social scene she'd grown weary of.

"Oh, I'm not glum," said Leo. "I'm just walking the ducks."

LillyAnn Pompadore had an unidentifiable animal fur wrapped around her neck, wore lots of make-up and carried a tiny dog under one arm. Leo could not help wondering how the dog must feel about the fur draped around its owner, but he kept silent, staring at the pond and hoping he could avoid a long conversation with the perpetually bored Ms Pompadore. The dog's name was Hiney, and he would sooner bite someone's hand than allow the slightest bit of petting. He also had the annoying habit of pooping in the hotel hallways, which didn't seem to bother Ms Pompadore in the slightest. This would set off the alarm in the basement with a ticker tape from Pilar, with a message that usually said something along the lines of *Hiney Alert. Clean up on Floor 7.*

Hiney started barking. He wasn't a fan of Betty and her clan, but they were safely in the water, so Leo didn't mind when Ms Pompadore set the little dog down and let him run around the pond as if he'd lost his mind.

"I do hope Mr Whippet will come back soon," Ms Pompadore drawled, fanning herself in the morning sun with a fashion magazine. "Where do you suppose he's gone off to?"

Leo shrugged, still hoping he could avoid a long encounter with a bored socialite.

"Well, no matter," she said. "Still, it's a very odd thing the way he disappeared like that. Do you suppose he's all right?"

"I'm sure he is," Leo answered without even thinking. But the thought had crossed his mind that Merganzer had almost never left the hotel grounds. How would he do out in the real world?

"He built this place," Ms Pompadore said, looking back at the off-kilter hotel. "Like the Leaning Tower of Pisa . . . and that thing's been standing for almost a thousand years. Maybe he knows something we don't."

"I'm sure he does," said Leo, always the first to come to Mr Whippet's defence.

Ms Pompadore called for Hiney and picked him up.

"Hiney and the ducks don't see eye to eye. I think I'll keep walking. Good luck with Betty."

Leo watched as LillyAnn Pompadore walked along the winding path towards the hotel. Then his eye caught sight of Mr Phipps out by the main gate. A black town car was pulling away, merging into a busy New York street.

"This is an odd day," said Leo, not talking to anyone in particular, though Betty honked from the pond as if she agreed.

Leo watched as Ms Sparks appeared at the gate as well, having come from the hotel. He couldn't hear what was being said, but it was obvious from her gestures that she wanted Mr Phipps away from the gate and back to work in the garden.

Leo gathered the ducks, his heart racing, and walked back to the lobby. It was all he could do not to pull their waddling bottoms behind him, because ducks were very slow about their business. It could take quite a while to get them back into the duck elevator.

Unfortunately, Ms Sparks left the main gate and headed for the hotel at precisely the same moment Leo left the pond. She went by a different winding path, but emerged from behind a series of carved animal bushes right as Leo arrived at the hotel.

"I hope you've got them under control this time," she said. "A new guest arrives this afternoon – thanks to me, we're actually booking some of these outrageously expensive rooms."

It was true that the Whippet usually had few guests besides the three long-stays, but things had indeed picked up a bit in Merganzer's absence. Ms Sparks seemed unable to help singing her own praises as she stared down at Betty with a sour look on her face.

"Mr Whippet didn't know the first thing about Internet marketing. It's the new frontier. Just keep Betty happy and we'll be fine. The last thing we need is the daughter of an oil tycoon getting bitten by a duck."

Ms Sparks brushed past Remi without a word, flicking a tiny feather off the shoulder of his red jacket as she passed by.

Leo stopped short this time and put out his hand.

"I'm Leo. I guess you're Remi."

"Oh, I know who you are," Remi replied. "My mum told me everything about this place. You and your dad keep it running."

Remi shook Leo's hand enthusiastically, as if he'd stood too long at the door and had pent-up energy ready to burn.

"Remi – that's an odd name," said Leo. "Short for Remington?"

Remi shook his head and said, a little too loudly,

"Short for Remilio. That was my mum's dad, but only my mum calls me that now. I like Remi."

"Okay, Remi, well, I gotta go." Leo was dying to get back to the box. "Have fun hanging out with Ms Sparks."

Remi gave Leo a look that said *Yeah, she's a barrel of laughs*, then leaned in close to his new friend and whispered.

"Whatever it is, it's got your name on it."

"What has?" asked Leo, but Remi wouldn't answer as Ms Sparks looked up and glared as though she might glue their mouths shut.

Leo didn't want a repeat of what had happened an hour before in the lobby, so he kept marching with Merganzer's walking stick until he reached the duck elevator, ignoring Remi's strange comment.

The miniature elevator wasn't parked on the roof, as he'd expected. Someone had called it back down to the lobby. He turned back to Remi, who smiled knowingly.

Uh-oh.

Remi didn't know much about the hotel. He was new and landlocked in the lobby. But he *had* managed to discover something secret in the duck elevator while Ms Sparks was out at the gate and walking in the grounds.

Leo opened the duck elevator and crawled inside, where he found that Remi was right.

The purple box didn't just have Merganzer's head on it. There were two words on the box as well, words that had been covered by a feather before, but were now clear as day.

For Leo

———

Bernard sat in the back seat of the black town car as Milton raced through town, speeding past taxis on an errand of the highest importance.

"I think this will do just fine," Bernard said as he watched the world race by. "Wouldn't you agree?"

"Oh yes," said Milton, pulling to a stop at a red light and staring into the rear-view mirror. "I think we've got the right person for the job."

"Let's hope so."

Milton riffled through his silver briefcase and removed a file folder.

"The files you were asking about? This is the first. It wasn't easy to find, let me tell you."

"Thank you, Milton. I do believe this is going to turn out marvellously."

Bernard Frescobaldi took the folder as the car

lurched forwards. They would be driving for a while, plenty of time to read more about Merganzer D Whippet. Bernard knew he had to understand the man's past in order to complete his plan. There were clues here, he was sure. He knew how rare these documents were, how hard they must have been to find. They could prove useless in the end, these old papers, but they could also reveal a clue that would help him get what he wanted.

Merganzer D Whippet, upon my father's death

I will not date these entries, for dates have only marked bad things in my life. I vow never to think of dates and days and times again. Here are some reasons why:

My mother died when I was four, a very bad day. I have many memories of her, though I've never written any of them down. That must change.

My father sent me to boarding school when I was a little bit bigger, also a bad day.

There were all the days in between when I wished my father would notice me, but he never did. On one of those days I made stilts that bounced up and down on springs, my first good invention, which my father ignored. They poked holes in the ceiling of my room, but what did it matter? My father had thousands of ceilings all over the city in all of his fancy hotels. Couldn't he do with one ceiling that had holes in it?

And finally there is today, the day my father died.

He leaves me with two things: a billion-dollar fortune, and a final verdict.

I will make wacky things, and I will be good at it.

A treasure and a curse, I suppose. But I am left with one thing more, something I don't think my father meant to leave behind.

I have a feeling it will matter most.

MDW

Note about my mother: she loved rings. I must make an effort to find all the rings I can.

Bernard searched the sky with his dancing eyes, nodding his head with assurance as he closed the folder. He had big plans for the hotel and the vast area of land it sat on, and more information than anyone else who might be trying to bring these things under their control.

"What are you hiding, Mr Whippet?" he asked.

· CHAPTER 3 ·

MR POWELL EXPLAINS THE RULES

The elevator had been so crammed with ducks on the way up to the roof that Leo couldn't properly examine the purple box. He'd counted the minutes while the elevator rose ever so slowly. Betty had held a sideways gaze on Leo, as if she was sure he was hiding more snacks, and now he felt glad to be going back down, alone at last with a box that had his name on it.

There were many ways into the maintenance tunnels of the Whippet Hotel, one of which required stopping between floors in the duck elevator. This Leo did, pulling the lever to the middle position just two minutes into the ride. The duck elevator stopped and

Leo turned a latch on the roof, popping it open to the shaft above. The opening wasn't very big, but it was large enough for Leo to slide the wooden box through and set it carefully to the side. Leo climbed through the opening as well and realized he'd stopped late. The round hole to the maintenance tunnel was almost out of reach, but not quite. Leo stretched up and pushed the purple box into the darkness of the tunnel.

His walkie-talkie squawked into life.

"Leo, come in. You there?"

It was his father. Leo's heart sank. He pulled the walkie-talkie from its latch and clicked the red button.

"Yeah, I'm here. Coming down from the roof."

He stared up at the large hole and wished he hadn't once again let the box out of his sight.

"New short-stays on six say the AC isn't working," his father reported. "Can you double back?"

Leo rolled his eyes. The air conditioning on the sixth floor worked fine; it just had an unusual way of turning on that Ms Sparks never wanted to explain.

"I'm on it. Give me five minutes."

"Perfect. After that, head over to that water leak in tunnel number eight. I'll be there working on the pipes."

"See you when I get there," said Leo. He was

between floors four and five, but there were ladders he could use in the tunnel system to get where he needed to go. Best to stay with the box if he could, so he didn't lose it.

Leo reached down into the elevator and pulled up on the lever, feeling himself move slowly upward. When the opening to the maintenance tunnel was thirty centimetres away, he jumped in. Turning back, Leo flipped the top shut on the elevator and heard it snap closed, then watched it go by on its way back to the roof.

Finally, he had a chance to sit in the light of the twisting tunnels and get a look inside the box. It took only a moment for Leo to discover he could slide off the top, which he did. What he saw made him gasp with delight.

"Where in the world is this place?" he whispered to himself. Looking inside the box was sort of like staring into a house with the roof torn off. There were walls and rooms and curves, and he could peer inside and see it all. From the top, the walls made a rat's maze of five circles, each circle smaller than the last. There were round rooms inside, too, growing smaller as they neared the centre. Closer and closer to the centre the circles went, but that wasn't all. All the pathways were filled with brightly coloured hoops of different shapes and sizes, turned at different angles. It was a marvel of ingenuity – intricate and perfect – and yet totally wacky.

Is it a ring of rooms or a room of rings? Leo wondered. *I think it must be both at once. How odd.*

Leo was leaning in for a closer inspection, pointing his standard-issue torch into the purple box, when his walkie-talkie came to life again. This time it was Ms Sparks.

She was in a bad temper.

"Leo Fillmore, if you're in the building, pick up. NOW."

He wanted desperately to turn off the walkie-talkie and figure out what the Room of Rings or the Ring of Rooms was supposed to mean. Why on earth had it shown up in a box with his name on it?

Leo pushed the button on the walkie-talkie.

"I'm heading to six now. Just need a few minutes more."

"You haven't fixed that AC problem yet?" yelled Ms Sparks, her voice bouncing off the tunnel walls. "Do you realize who's in there? He's worth about a zillion dollars and his daughter gets very ratty in the heat. If she's ratty, HE'S ratty. Get on it, Fillmore!"

"Almost there," Leo said.

"And get back to the lobby the moment you're done. Remi needs a toilet break and YOU need to watch the door. There's been too much mischief around here lately."

What did she mean by mischief? Was it the black town car or the ducks in the lobby, or something else? Whatever the reason, Ms Sparks was on the alert, and Leo took that as a bad sign.

He couldn't believe how busy his day was getting. AC units, water pipes, door duty, duck walking – his head was spinning as he grabbed the purple lid and saw what he hadn't seen before. On the underside was taped a fancy envelope. A message had been written above the envelope, on the wood of the box itself, in Merganzer's big and round writing, which Leo recognized instantly.

Floor and three and one half!
Strike the purple ball in the kitchen by the hall.
Three times fast. Duck!
And bring the ball. You'll need it.

Leo felt an immediate sense of goodwill and comfort. Merganzer D Whippet only spoke in such strange turns of phrase when he was at his happiest, like when they were flying up the Double Helix and he would scream, "Dancing sharks go jumping Bob!" Mr Whippet was the smartest man Leo had ever met *most* of the time, but his happiness brought out a wild glee that tumbled out of his mouth like sweets.

Floor and three and one half had an authentic Whippet ring to it.

"LEOOOOOOOOOO!" Ms Sparks screamed into the walkie-talkie.

Leo turned the volume dial down, her voice growing quieter, as if she were falling down an elevator shaft.

He turned his attention to the fancy envelope, carefully pulling it free from the lid of the purple box. Time stood still for Leo as he opened and read the note. No thoughts of a zillionaire with a ratty daughter. No Ms Sparks or leaky pipes.

There was only the letter and the box.

Young Mr Fillmore,

If you are in receipt of this letter, then Mr Whippet has been gone for exactly one hundred days. As his long time personal friend and attorney, I have been instructed to set things in motion.

I am only allowed to tell you four things:

– There are four boxes, all of which must be found.

– There are two days, including this one. That is all the time you have.

– You may enlist the help of only one other, preferably a child.

– Always bring a duck if you can. They are more useful than you know. If you can't find a duck, bring a friend. Never go it alone.

Don't fail, young Mr Fillmore, for if you do, the Whippet Hotel and all it stands for will come to an end.

Only you can save the Whippet now. He's counting on you to set things right.

Thoughtfully yours,

George Powell

Attorney at Law

1 Park Avenue West, 44th floor, door number four

New York

Leo felt the weight of the entire hotel resting on his shoulders. Was it really up to him, a ten-year-old boy, to save the hotel? And what did four weird boxes have to do with saving a hotel, anyway?

He looked at the walkie-talkie, the red light blinking on and off: Ms Sparks or his father, no doubt.

He'd stayed too long exploring the purple box of rings. Leo put the fancy envelope and the letter in the front pocket of his overalls and started to put the lid back on the box. As he did, he heard his father's voice echoing down the maintenance tunnel.

"Leo? You in there?"

Leo slid the cover of the box quietly until it was firmly back in place. Then he picked it up, searching for a place to hide it before his father came lumbering around a corner. The tunnel was narrow but tall, filled with all sorts of pipes and meters, and it snaked all the way around the building in a complete circle. This was one of the oddities of the Whippet Hotel: it was true that there were nine floors, but there was a lot of space between each floor. The tunnels ran all through many of those sections, with ladder tubes here and there between the floors the guests stayed on. Leo had long since memorized every nook and cranny of the tunnel system, and one thing was abundantly clear: there was no place to hide a purple box where his father wouldn't see it.

Leo looked in every direction and realized he had only one choice if he wanted to keep the secret safe.

By the time Clarence Fillmore arrived at the small

round opening that led to the duck elevator, his son was gone.

And so was the box.

Carrying a box down a ladder is easier said than done, and Leo nearly dropped it more than once as he descended from the fifth floor to the fourth. He wound his way through the fourth floor tunnel lined with pipes, some of them shooting steam with a loud hissing sound as he passed by. Another hole with a ladder appeared, and down he went again, arriving in the maintenance tunnel on the third floor. Five minutes later, he arrived back in the basement boiler room, where he tucked the purple box under his bed for safe keeping. He was already out of breath, but he climbed all the way back up to six in order to set the AC that Ms Sparks couldn't figure out.

"Don't tell me you didn't have a signal," Ms Sparks screamed when he finally returned to the lobby, her beehive cone of hair dancing back and forth over his head. "Remi nearly peed his pants!"

Leo couldn't understand why she hadn't let Remi leave for what would amount to a two-minute break, but he wasn't about to ask her in the mood she was in.

"And you took for ever fixing the air conditioning on six," Ms Sparks continued as Remi hopped off in the direction of the toilet. "What if the Yanceys decide they don't want to stay here after all? What then? How do you think Mr Whippet will feel about *that* when he gets back? Well? Say something!"

Leo cleared his throat. He hadn't caught the name of the girl or her parents as he'd flipped the AC switch up, down, and up again, then turned the temperature dial all the way to zero and back to nineteen degrees. Once it had turned on, the girl plonked herself down in front of the cold air and stared at Leo as if he was a pile of stinky dirt.

"You know, Ms Sparks, the AC unit in that room isn't that complicated. Should I explain it to you one more time?"

Ms Sparks's face looked as though she was trying to make fireworks shoot out of her ears. She hated it when she couldn't figure out how the hotel worked, which was practically all the time.

"I'm reporting you, Leo Fillmore. Don't say I didn't warn you."

Being reported by Ms Sparks had an uncertain meaning. Leo had been reported dozens of times, but what happened to these reports was a mystery. He had a feeling they went into her desk as evidence for a future trial of his skills and character at a time of her choosing.

When Remi whizzed back through the lobby looking relieved, Ms Sparks was on the phone having a long conversation with Ms Pompadore about where to get the best hats in Manhattan.

"Thanks, Leo, I needed that." Remi sighed. "Did you meet the zillionaire's daughter? She's a real charmer."

"I fixed the air conditioning, which seemed to make her happy." Leo kept his voice to a whisper, and signalled to Remi to do the same. The smaller boy adjusted the red trousers and bow tie of his uniform and tried to play it cool. "But I think that little kid is going to give us some trouble. She's a bad-tempered six-year-old and she's bored. Bad combo."

"I hear you, man." The zillionaire's kid was named Jane Yancey, and Remi ticked off her attributes on his fingers. "Jane Yancey: six years old, bored, spoilt. *Super-size* bad combo."

"Listen, Remi, I might need your help on a few things this week. Can I count on you?"

Remi's face lit up. He was dying to escape the company of Ms Sparks and explore the Whippet Hotel.

"Does it have anything to do with that box? The purple one?"

Remi was curious, but he was also new to the hotel. Leo could use this to his advantage.

"Nah, it's just something I use to work with the ducks."

"Ooooh, right. Like duck food and stuff."

"Right, duck food."

Remi was all smiles.

"*Anything* I can do that gets me away from this door, I'm in. Just say the word."

Leo was starting to think this might work out okay. Having someone to cover for him in a pinch could really come in handy. He'd brought his bag full of hotel tools with him and opened it up just as Ms Sparks covered the receiver and yelled across the lobby.

"Don't you have some pipes to fix?"

"Yes, ma'am. I'm on my way."

"Good. Stop on floor three on the way. Hiney did a hoo-hoo."

"Who calls a dog poop a *hoo-hoo*?" Remi whispered, shaking his head.

"Take this," Leo said, handing Remi one of two small radios he'd picked up weeks ago from a street vendor. "I've got one, too, and both are set to frequency number four. If you hear a little beep, it's me."

Remi's eyes grew big and he smiled at Leo.

"Partners?" he dared to ask.

"Partners," said Leo.

CHAPTER 4

INTO THE PINBALL MACHINE

It was a beautiful summer night in the grounds, where Mr Phipps had surrounded the carved hedges and giant bushes around the pond with tiny lights that shone like stars. The ducks had been brought down and swam lazily in the water, quacking softly at the setting sun, although Betty was not among them.

"Dinner is served," said Ms Sparks, playing hostess to the guests who'd chosen to attend the party. This included a smattering of short-stays, including Jane Yancey, the stroppy little daughter of the zillionaire, and her mother, Nancy Yancey. The father, presumably, had business to attend to on Wall Street.

Ms Pompadore was there with Hiney, who sat by the pond barking at the ducks.

Meanwhile, Captain Rickenbacker was deep in conversation with Mr Phipps about the shapes of the bushes.

"I want a duck," said little Jane Yancey, who wouldn't leave the edge of the pond to come to the table.

"Ask your father," replied her mother.

"Do you want to cook the duck or put it on a leash?" asked Ms Pompadore, who had no patience whatsoever with spoilt children.

Jane ran to the table and sat by her mother, complaining about the rude woman and her barking dog, and dinner was served.

There was no main kitchen in the hotel, but it didn't matter. Dinner, along with every other meal at the Whippet, was cooked by one of the finest restaurants in New York, one street away from the property. The restaurant was owned by the Whippet estate, and it only served the hotel. If you had a yellow or green key card, you could dine there any time of the day or night and never pay a penny. (Tips were also discouraged.) Or guests could ring the restaurant by inserting a key card into a dining slot in their rooms, and food would be delivered to their doors under silver domes on piping hot plates. The staff was not invited to dine with guests, unless you were Ms Sparks.

And so it was that Leo had eaten dinner in the basement – a bowl of noodles and a banana – while he'd stared into the purple box. His father was off in the expanse of the maintenance tunnels, working on something or other, when Leo made the call.

"Remi, are you there?"

A split second later Remi answered, as if he'd been holding the two-way radio next to his face, waiting for it to go off.

"I'm here! Where are you?"

"That's not important now. Who's in the lobby?"

"Me and my mum. Your dad came through on his way up a while ago, but otherwise, it's been quiet."

"Do you know where Captain Rickenbacker is?"

"I do. He's at the dinner party by the pond in the grounds."

"Good! He went as I'd hoped."

There was a leather string tied to his belt notch, and Leo pulled it out, staring at a tiny watch that was attached to the end. Betty was busy gobbling up half of Leo's dinner while he talked, a stray noodle hanging from her bill.

"I've got Betty with me, and I'll need to return her and the rest of the ducks to the roof in just under an hour. In the meantime, I've got an errand to run. Call me if Captain Rickenbacker comes back, will you?"

"Of course I will!"

———

Remi had let himself grow too enthusiastic, and his mother looked up from behind the desk, where she was filing her nails.

"You must be hungry, no?" she asked.

She smiled and called Remi to the desk, where she gave him a slice of cold pizza wrapped in wax paper.

"You make me proud, my little doorman. Keep working hard and you'll make your way in the world."

Remi went back to the door with one hand in his pocket, secretly holding the two-way radio in case Leo needed him. In his other hand he held his dinner, which was a repeat of what he'd had for lunch.

Hearing the distant sound of ducks quacking on the pond, he gazed out over the grounds and wondered what Leo and Betty were doing.

———

There were two ways into Captain Rickenbacker's

room on the third floor – one in the hallway and one in the maintenance tunnel. Not all the rooms were designed this way, but there had been some problems over the past two years in that room, so Mr Whippet had shown Leo a secret way in. Captain Rickenbacker had a habit of pushing large pieces of furniture in front of the door and refusing to come out, which was usually because his arch-nemesis, Mr M, had entered the hotel. Mr M was, as far as the hotel staff could tell, a figment of Captain Rickenbacker's imagination. It was usually Leo's dad who was sent in to reassure the Captain and move the furniture away from the door so that Pilar could clean the room.

Leo looked down at Betty. "Be careful in here, okay? It's really no place for a duck."

Betty didn't seem to be paying attention as Leo spun the combination lock on the secret door from the maintenance tunnel. On the room side, it looked as if part of the wall were swinging open, and when the door was closed again, it would look like there was no door at all. Betty waddled through the opening, and Leo, holding the purple box under one arm, followed her. He was careful not to let the door shut all the way, marvelling at one of the most danger-ous rooms in the hotel.

"It looks like fun, but really, it's a duck killer. Be *super* careful, Betty."

She honked, nodded her head and waddled forwards.

Captain Rickenbacker stayed in a large and colourful room known as the Pinball Machine. The Pinball Machine had windows high up on the walls, from which the setting sun cast a golden glow over all the parts and pieces.

"I've always liked this room," said Leo. He was tempted to set the purple box down and play one of the twenty-three pinball machines that lined the bedroom wall, but he knew his time was limited. It would require some luck getting into the Ring of Rooms as it was, so there was no time for fooling around. The last thing he needed was for Captain Rickenbacker to return, thinking this little kid in his room was a manifestation of his made-up arch-enemy, Mr M. If that happened, Captain Rickenbacker might go bananas and start throwing things. And there were some dangerous, heavy things to throw in the Pinball Machine.

Leo walked into the main room, which was long and narrow in the same way that a pinball machine was. This was the centrepiece of the Pinball Machine, with giant moulded pinball bumpers that doubled as couches and chairs, all of them lit up with bright lights and springs. The slanted floor was covered in lights and arrows and circled numbers, just like a real pinball machine. At the far end of the room was a hole as big as a tyre, which had a flipper on each side. Behind that was the doorway that led to the third-floor landing.

Betty waddled down the room and honked into the hole, listening to the echo as Leo looked around. While he'd eaten dinner next to the glugging boiler in the basement, he'd reread Merganzer's message, searching for clues.

Floor and three and one half!

This, he was sure, meant to say there were hidden rooms in the hotel, and one of them was above the third floor and below the fourth. He was now standing in the Pinball Machine, which was on the third floor, staring at the ceiling and wondering what was up there.

Strike the purple ball in the kitchen by the hall.

Leo walked down the polished, slanted floor, careful not to slip, and arrived at the control booth. He set the box down, and found himself feeling happy about the fact that the purple ball was stuck under a blue ball. They were big, like bowling balls, and just about as heavy. The blue ball would have to be played in order to retrieve the purple one from the track. In fact, the purple ball would need to be played as well, because the balls were stacked under a sheet of thick Plexiglas. They were only dangerous after they were shot into play. After that, a person could really get hurt in the Pinball Machine, which was definitely why Ms Sparks was so happy Captain Rickenbacker had stayed in the room so long. No one else would rent it.

"Betty," said Leo, "we'll need to play a couple of balls. Stay in here with me, okay?"

Betty didn't mind being picked up – in fact, she loved it. When Leo put one hand on each side and lifted her up so she could stand near the controls, she sighed happily.

Leo pulled back on the giant spring-loaded ball whacker and let go, sending the blue ball up the silver rails and into play. It bounced off spring-loaded couches and chairs, spun through a whirligig and headed for one of the two giant flippers. The room was alive with bells and zingers, lights blinking everywhere. Betty was mesmerized, concentrating on every move the ball made. Leo had planned to simply let the ball bounce off the flipper and land in the gutter, but he couldn't help himself. He simply had to slap the flipper buttons with the palms of his hands (the buttons were big, like dinner plates) and send the blue ball sailing back up towards the kitchen, where it knocked down several letters that spelled out *MERGANZER*. The back wall spun the score on white tiles with black numbers as the ball came flying back towards the control booth. It slammed into a bumper and took flight, crashing into thick Plexiglas in front of Leo's face. Leo aughed nervously, thinking to himself, *If not for the Plexiglas, that ball would have knocked my block off.*

Betty honked nervously, flapping her wings in the small space.

"Just stay put and you'll be fine."

He let the blue ball drop into the tyre-sized hole, then shot the purple ball into play. This was where it would get dangerous, because he needed that ball. He'd have to go out and get it.

Okay, Leo, you can do this. Just take it slowly.

"You wait here," he told Betty, giving her a stern look that she returned with equal vigour. Betty didn't like to be bossed.

The ball was bouncing wildly back and forth between two chairs as Leo jumped out from behind the safety of the control room. He was standing in the middle of a live pinball machine, wondering what it would feel like to catch a bowling ball going fifty miles per hour. The ball came free from the back-and-forth of the bumpers and down the floor at lightning speed. Leo dived out of the way, sliding into a bumper of his own and feeling it fling him back like a rag doll. As he got his bearings, Leo saw that the ball had bounced back up in an arc. He turned and jumped, catching the ball in the guts as it knocked him to the slippery floor. The weight of the ball pulled Leo down towards a round hole that would try to swallow him up. But Leo was a fast thinker, even inside a giant pinball machine. He held the ball in his arms, spread his legs, and caught hold of one flipper with each foot. If Betty were to walk on to one of the flipper buttons in the control booth, he might not live to tell about it, and he watched the duck carefully.

Betty quacked. She stared at Leo, then at the big white buttons.

"Betty, no. Please, don't –"

She held one webbed foot over the right flipper button, paused, then slammed it down.

Leo leaned over to the left flipper just in time, but Betty was laughing now, waddling back and forth between the flippers as if it were the most fun she'd ever had in her life.

It took four or five jumps back and forth before Leo dived past the gutter and landed against the door with a thud.

"That wasn't nice," he chided the duck, standing up with the bowling ball in his arms.

His secret two-way radio squawked into life.

"Remi here. Leo, you there?"

Remi was whispering. Not a good sign. Leo pulled out the tiny watch on the string – twenty minutes gone already!

"I'm here. What's up?"

"Nothing much. I'm bored. What are you doing?"

Leo thought about what he should say. Remi was still brand-new and he barely knew him. What if he told him a crazy duck was trying to kill him inside a giant pinball machine?

He settled for something slightly less weird.

"I can't talk now – I'm dodging bowling balls. Don't

call unless Rickenbacker is coming up here. Got it?"

"Do you have any idea how tedious it is standing at this door? You're dodging bowling balls and my brain cells are melting from boredom. You've gotta get me in the game!"

"Not now, Remi! Stay focused. We'll talk about this later."

Leo moved his plan on to the next stage, setting Betty on the pinball floor and running up to the kitchen with the purple ball under one arm and the box under the other. He could barely hold on to both and nearly dropped the ball twice, which would have meant playing the whole thing out again and probably getting flipped around the room by an unreliable duck.

He got to the kitchen and saw the spot he was looking for: a wall of lights in the shapes of bowling balls. One of them was purple, and Leo felt sure he knew what to do.

Strike the purple ball in the kitchen by the hall.
Three times fast. Duck!

He set the box down on the counter, careful not to let it touch a bumper. Then he held the heavy purple ball in front of the round light and shoved. When the ball hit the light it kept right on going, right through the wall, and dropped out of sight. Then the light was back.

"Uh-oh," said Leo. "I don't think that was supposed to happen."

Betty quacked from the floor and Leo looked down. The ball was back, rolling out of a different hole by his feet.

"I guess I should do it three times, right?" he asked Betty.

Betty just stared at the refrigerator, which was shaped like a huge flipper standing on end.

When Leo picked up the ball, it was half as heavy.

"Different ball. Interesting."

He shoved it at the light again, and again it melted into the wall, dropped out of sight and appeared at his feet. This time it was a lot lighter, like an over-sized golf ball.

"Is it just me, or is this getting more confusing by the minute?"

The one-way conversation with Betty was surprisingly calming, and Leo began to think maybe he was more like Merganzer than he'd even thought. Merganzer loved talking but didn't often want anyone talking back. Leo was like that, too. Speaking helped him think clearly, and ducks were awfully good listeners.

"One more time and I bet this thing will float away."

Leo passed the ball through the hole one last time, and when he did, Betty honked louder than Leo had ever heard her honk before.

He was reminded in that split second of one very important word in Merganzer's note.

Duck!

In this particular case, his mind flashed a message: *Merganzer probably wasn't talking about a real duck. He probably meant* you're *supposed to duck.*

Not one to take chances, Leo ducked, and when he did, the original purple ball (the one that felt like a bowling ball) flew out of the hole in the wall and back into the pinball machine where it belonged. It careered through a flipping turnstile near the ceiling, an impossible shot from any other angle, and all the lights in the room went dark. The ball bounced loudly down into the gutter, and when it was gone, the lights came up a dark purple. A deep hum filled the room as a hole slid open in the ceiling and a white light shone down on the dark surface of the floor.

A ladder descended.

Leo had popped back up when the ball flew past his head, and had watched the pinball machine change. Now he was back on the floor, crouching down as another purple ball rolled out and bumped lazily against his foot. Leo took a moment to thank Betty for saving his life, then picked up the fourth ball. It felt like a ping-pong ball. Leo dropped it and it bounced right back up with a hollow sound.

Leo thought of the other words Merganzer had written on the box.

And bring the ball. You'll need it.

"All right, I will," said Leo.

He started walking towards the ladder, worried and nervous, as Remi's voice blasted out of the two-way radio.

"Captain Rickenbacker is on the move! He's heading your way!"

Leo had turned the room a deep shade of neon purple and opened a hole in the ceiling in the space of half an hour. He had no idea how to make everything go back to the way it was.

So he did what any kid would do: he threw the ball and the duck up into the hole, grabbed the purple box and climbed up the ladder.

· CHAPTER 5 ·

THE ROOM OF RINGS
OR THE RING OF ROOMS

When Captain Rickenbacker placed his yellow key card into the slot for his room, he heard an unexpected sequence of sounds: a *swoosh*, a *slam* and a charge of electric energy. He jumped back from the door as if it were covered in Kryptonite (he considered himself distantly related to Superman).

"Mr M, I presume," he whispered, for he was sure his enemy was inside rigging all sorts of traps in his beloved Pinball Machine.

If Captain Rickenbacker could have seen what was happening on the other side of the door, it would have almost surely confirmed his suspicions.

The ladder shot back from where it had come

with stunning speed. The round door in the ceiling slammed shut. The lights in the Pinball Machine went back to the way they had been before.

The Captain's key card had activated a fail-safe to the Ring of Rooms.

Stealth was not one of Captain Rickenbacker's strong suits. He was more inclined to bold attacks and ninja moves. And so it was that he burst open the door and started shooting bowling balls into the room one right after the other, yelling all the while: "Take that! And that! And that!"

Leo was alone on floor three and one half in an airtight room. There was no noise from above or below. Both the secret two-way radio and his walkie-talkie had lost their signals. He could not hear Captain Rickenbacker trying with all his superhero might to flush out Mr M. The only noise Leo could hear was Betty's soft breathing, which was very soft indeed.

"I think it's time I opened the box again," Leo said. Betty didn't quack, but she seemed to approve of the idea, and Leo slid the cover off, staring inside. Over dinner he had worked out that the lid would slide on to the back of the box as well, and this he did so as not to leave it behind if he got lost in the maze.

"I think I'm standing right here," he said, setting the box and the very large purple ping-pong ball on the floor next to him. He was pointing to a small, round mark on the floor of the model while Betty waddled off behind him.

The box was full of coloured rings of different sizes, and so was the room. All the walls in the real room were bright white, lit from behind frosty glass. And all the rings were positioned exactly where they were in the box. The advantage of having the box, it seemed to Leo, was that he knew how to navigate the complex maze before him.

Betty quacked from further away than Leo was comfortable with. She was a mischievous companion, known to wander off on her own, and he felt sure she was about to somehow open the door and send the ladder back into the room below. But when he looked over his shoulder, he saw that she was simply staring at a white wall of frosty glass, where a message had started to appear. Leo took three steps towards her through the only ringless space in the whole maze and watched as the words appeared. It was as if someone were behind the glass, writing on a foggy window with his finger.

Did you bring the ball?
Make it fly, make it fall.
  Mr M

Something fell out of the ceiling, missing Betty by a whisker, and a dark shadow moved behind the glass. Leo jumped back, afraid of something in the Whippet Hotel for the first time in his life.

He wasn't alone in the Room of Rings, as he'd supposed. And what was more frightening still: Mr M wasn't a figment of someone's imagination. He was real.

Maybe Captain Rickenbacker wasn't totally off his rocker after all.

Leo gathered his nerves and picked up what had fallen out of the ceiling. It looked as if it had been designed to work with the box. It had a metal platform and two handles sticking out, like the handles of a motorcycle. He took up the box and placed it carefully on top of the square platform between the handles. A perfect fit, if ever there was one. A new sound rose from behind him – the sound of wind. When Leo turned, the giant purple ping-pong ball had floated up into the air.

"I know what I'm supposed to do!" he said excitedly. "I understand!"

Leo told Betty to stay right behind him and to do exactly as he did, and somehow he knew she'd understood. She fell in line as Leo held the handles on the box and stared into the model.

"I know the way out of here, but there must be some trick to it, and the trick must involve the ball."

As he neared the floating ball, he felt what he'd expected: a strong channel of air was coming out of the floor, holding up the ball. Leo twisted the right handle as if he were actually riding a motorcycle and watched as the ball moved slowly forwards. Twisting it the other way brought the ball right back. He tilted the front edge of the box down and the ball descended, the flow of air from the floor growing weaker. Then he tilted the front of the box up faster than he should have and the ball bounced off the ceiling. He levelled the box, and the ball was back, holding steady in front of his eyes.

"Well, Betty, I know how to get this ball through the maze. I just don't know why I'm doing it."

Leo shrugged. There was nothing to be done but guide the ball and follow it through, and so he began. Everything started out fine, twisting and turning through one green, then one yellow, then two red rings, Betty hopping through the rings behind him.

But then he came to a place in the round maze where there were two rings to choose from. They were in the opening that would send him deeper into the maze, closer to the middle and the very end. Would it matter which one he chose? He thought not, and sent the ball through the blue ring on the right. When he did, the ring filled with spires of electricity and the ball exploded into dust.

Leo lurched back, nearly falling into one of the rings, and stared in shock at the purple dust particles flying every where. If there were such a thing as fairy dust, Leo thought, it would look like this. The electric charge had turned the ball into sparkling purple mist that stuck in Leo's round tuft of hair and danced on the wind.

He tried to calm himself down, but could only imagine what would happen to him if he went through the wrong ring. Would he, too, be turned to dust, never to escape the Ring of Rooms or the Room of Rings?

"At least now I know what the purple ball was for," he said. "But it's gone now."

Leo was aware of the time ticking away, and this only added to his anxiety. Checking his watch, he saw that he'd already been gone a full hour. Ms Sparks would be furious about the ducks being left in the pond. Then she'd find that Betty was missing and go ballistic. And what about his father – what would he say if Leo couldn't be found?

Leo was looking at Betty as though she might have the answer to all his problems, but it turned out she had the key to a different question. She was staring at one of the frosty glass walls again, watching a new message appear. Leo joined her as an unseen finger wrote out seven words before the shadow moved off again.

Turn the handle back three times fast.

Leo was beside himself with worry, but he couldn't give up now. For starters, he didn't know how to get the round door back open again. And even if he could get it open, there would be Captain Rickenbacker and his flying bowling balls to deal with.

He turned the handle back once, a second time, then once more. A big blue ball, round and perfect, dropped out of the ceiling and was held on the wind in front of the two rings.

"I wonder how many of these I get," Leo said to

Betty, excited to have another ball but realizing he had to be extremely careful. If he got too far into the maze and ran out of balls, he might never get out. He'd have to remember exactly which rings were capable of turning him into fairy dust.

Leo twisted the handle forwards and sent the blue ball safely through the opening on the left, then stepped through himself. Betty flew carefully through the ring as well, and they were safely into the second circular layer of the maze. Looking at the model in the box, Leo saw many openings that led to the next inner level, but only one had an arrow pointing inside. He was excited again, less nervous, realizing that no one else but he could complete the maze and live to tell about it.

During the next twenty minutes, Leo blew up four more giant ping-pong balls on his way to the centre of the Room of Rings. He began to anticipate seeing them explode and felt less anxious when they did. Watching the orange ball blast into dust was particularly enjoyable, because orange was his favourite colour.

He couldn't have known, for there were no mirrors in the maze, but his hair was starting to look like a rainbow, dusted with purple, green, orange, yellow and blue as he arrived in the inner circle of the maze.

He'd exploded the green ball on the way into this chamber, and passing through the opening into the centre of the maze, he felt as if he were standing in the middle of an igloo. The walls were frosty white and perfectly round, curved into a dome at the top. He stood there with his box and his duck and wondered what he should do, for the room was completely empty.

The opening to the room, which he had just passed through, was suddenly gone, filled by a curved wall sliding down from above. Leo was trapped in a half circle of pure white, his heart beating faster as a terrible thought crossed his mind.

No one knows I'm here.

But that wasn't entirely true. There was one person who knew, and whoever it was began writing a message on the ceiling, just the way he'd written the other messages before.

"Is that you, Merganzer?" asked Leo, setting the purple box and the handles on the floor and reaching up towards the ceiling. "Won't you please come out?"

He'd had his suspicions, but there was no way he could know for sure. It was a dangerous path he'd taken to the white room, and it would be unlike his old friend to place him in harm's way. Then again, who else could it be, helping him along and pretending to be Mr M all this time?

It was a short message, only three words:

Take the ring.

At first the message made no sense, because there were no rings in the room to take. But then something small dropped through a hole in the ceiling. Quickly thrusting out his hand, Leo caught the object before it hit the floor.

There was a deep silence then. Even Betty seemed to understand that something important had just happened. Leo knew it, too, but he didn't say anything. There was something very special about the ring that had fallen into his hand. Something so special it nearly made him cry, but not quite, as he placed it in his pocket next to his mother's watch.

"Thank you, whoever you are."

Without any warning at all, the hole in the ceiling got bigger and a blue box fell through. It was exactly the same shape and size as the purple box sitting in the centre of the room. Leo caught the blue box as it was falling, finding it heavier than the purple box, but not by much. On the lid was a message.

Don't turn me upside down. Don't open me until morning.

The emblem of Merganzer's head was also on the box, right in the middle.

"I got another box," said Leo, very proud of himself for what he'd done. "What do you think of that, Betty?"

Betty was growing very bored and extremely hungry. She honked irritably, staring up at Leo as if to say *I've had it with rings and rooms and boxes. Get me to the roof or I'll chew on your shoes.*

"We *have* been in here a while, haven't we? But I don't know how to get out."

Leo wanted desperately to open the blue box, but he'd been told not to, so instead he took the purple box off the handles and set them aside. He put the lid back on the purple box and set the boxes next to each other.

And then he sat there for about a minute, unsure what to do, until a new message appeared on the ceiling.

Connect the boxes.
Pick them up.

Like all the earlier messages, this one appeared, then slowly drifted away, the frost returning to the glass.

It took only a moment for Leo to work out that the blue box slid snugly on top of the purple box on little wooden rails he hadn't paid any attention to before. The two were one now, inseparable unless they were intentionally slid apart.

There was one last message being drawn with a finger on the glass, and this one worried Leo greatly.

Hold on tight!

He didn't see any reason to hold on tight, so the message unnerved him. Should he hold the boxes tight, or pick up Betty and hold her tight, or was the floor about to fa—

The third thing Leo thought – the thought about the floor falling away – was the reason he was supposed to hold on tight. He found himself on a twisting slide and wondered if he was inside one of the tubes of the Double Helix. Those were far too narrow, he knew, but things had got so terribly strange at the Whippet Hotel that he couldn't tell up from down. Wherever he was, he was falling fast, turning sharply every few seconds, barely keeping hold of the two boxes that had become one. He came to a harrowing U-turn and was tossed from the tube, landing squarely on top of the duck elevator. He made the mistake of turning towards the echoing sound of Betty sliding down behind him, and she crashed into his face, feathers flying as she regained her webbed footing and quacked angrily.

Leo threw open the trapdoor on top of the duck elevator and jumped inside, landing with a bouncy *thud*. He grabbed the boxes first, then the duck, and shut himself inside.

"It's getting awfully crowded in here, wouldn't you say?" he asked Betty. Two boxes, a boy and a duck did take up some space when there wasn't much to be had.

There was plenty of good news, though, as the small elevator lurched to life and started its slow descent to the lobby. Leo was in possession of the second of four boxes. He was halfway to somewhere, though he had no idea where. He had a special ring in his pocket. And he was free of the Room of Rings or the Ring of Rooms, whichever it was called.

The bad news?

The walkie-talkie had started working again, and Ms Sparks was screaming at him.

———————————

Bernard Frescobaldi was back in the hotel across the street, staring at the huge, nearly empty site that held the Whippet Hotel. Something was troubling him.

"Milton, a cappuccino, if you please."

"Right away, sir. Right away."

Milton went to work at the rather elaborate coffee-making machine in the corner of the room. It had been brought over from Italy, along with Italian espresso beans, cups, saucers, spoons and a grinder. The room filled with the smells and sounds of good, strong coffee.

"Something's not right over there," said Bernard as Milton delivered the small red cup topped with foam.

"How do you mean, sir?"

Milton returned to the machine to make his own drink, for he knew his boss would take some time answering the question.

"Someone is set against us, though I can't see who," Bernard continued, still staring out of the window as Milton returned.

"I think our plan is going to work," Milton assured him, sipping carefully from his own cup. "How can we lose with you-know-who on the job?"

"True enough. Still, I can't help but want to stack the deck more in my favour. Read me that travel entry again, will you, Milton? I think it may be of some help."

Milton went to his silver briefcase, riffled through the contents, and found the entry in question. He sipped his strong coffee, cleared his throat, and began reading out loud.

Merganzer D Whippet, travelogue 3

I'm travelling with George once more, on the train between New York and Washington DC. George keeps telling me how much money I've got hold of and how hard it will be to spend it all. I keep reminding him I have plans equal to the task.

I've only ridden on two train lines, the one that leads to the boarding school in Pittsburgh and the one I'm on now. I adore one train, loathe the other, a true love/hate relationship.

No travel was ever so dreary as the train ride to and from the boarding school.

But the second train – the one I'm riding now – was mine and my mother's for a brief time. She'd been tired a lot for some reason, so I said we didn't have to go, but she insisted. Being five, I was all too happy to agree. We should go!

We took the train to the Smithsonian in Washington DC, and she pointed out all sorts of things along the way, which surprised me. When had she ever been out and about? I'd always imagined her folding my clothes and making my breakfast. Funny how I didn't realize how remarkable she was, how much she'd accomplished.

Dad had said of Washington, "Take him to the mint to watch them make money. It might teach him a thing or two," but my mother had other ideas. She liked rockets, history, art, music and especially robots. Or could it be, she knew I loved those things best, and wanted me to see them?

Either way, we never went back.

One time on the better train of the two was all I ever got.

After that, my mother was tired all the time. She hardly got out of bed, and I thought a terrible thought: our one great adventure had worn her out. I'd exhausted her.

MDW.

PS. I have a plan for a hotel, and in the hotel will be a Railway Room. I don't think I'll let anyone inside the Railway Room. At least not for a while.

Bernard shook his head.

Milton scrunched his nose. "I've been all through the place, top to bottom. There is no Railway Room. Right?"

"Either way, our plan is in motion. Things will get interesting, starting tomorrow." Milton sipped the last of his coffee. "I can hardly wait."

· CHAPTER 6 ·

THEODORE BUMP AND
THE TROUBLESOME ROBOT

By the time Leo reached the lobby, the hotel was ready for the night. Remi had fallen asleep in one of the big chairs while his mother quietly dusted the brass handrails. Ms Sparks was nowhere to be seen, off on a rampage searching for Leo all over the hotel.

Leo tucked the two boxes beneath the nearest sculpted green bush (it was in the shape of a rabbit) and turned to send the duck elevator back up to the roof. Betty was sitting down in it, nestled in a ball, which was very unlike her.

"Are you okay? You must be hungry."

Leo felt terrible. He loved animals, and he'd put Betty through quite an adventure. The poor thing could barely keep her eyes open.

"I'm sending you back to the roof now," Leo whispered. "You'll find some food in the pond."

He closed the duck elevator and pushed the button for the roof.

"Where've you been? Everyone's looking for you!"

Remi had woken and tiptoed over in the dim light of the lobby, scaring Leo half to death.

"Don't sneak up on me like that!"

"Sorry, it's a habit of mine. I like to sneak."

Remi's mop of dark hair was messy from sleep, and he'd loosened his kid-sized bow tie.

"Sneaking might come in handy," said Leo. "Just don't sneak up on *me*."

Remi smiled widely and stole a look back into the main lobby.

"I'm going to leave in a minute," he said, "but I'll be back in the morning. Can I keep the two-way radio?"

"Of course you can," said Leo. "You are my partner after all, right?"

Remi was growing on Leo, but more importantly, Leo was going to need his help in order to find all the boxes and get to the bottom of what was going on.

"I could sneak away from the door if you want," Remi offered.

"How?" asked Leo, assuming Ms Sparks's evil eye was on the door all day long.

"Ms Sparks has errands tomorrow afternoon, so my mum will be in charge of the front desk. She said she'd watch the door so I could explore if I wanted to, as long as I didn't go looking for cupcakes. Are there cupcakes up there?"

Remi looked up at the ceiling curiously, licking his lips.

"You've never been upstairs?" asked Leo. He had such free rein of the hotel, it hadn't occurred to him that others might not share the same privilege.

"Are you kidding? I've only been here one day, and I spend every waking moment standing at that dull front door. It's torture."

Remi looked at the ceiling again.

"How many cupcakes are up there?"

"Forget about the cupcakes, Remi. We've got more important things to think about. Right now I have to get these boxes to the basement and avoid Ms Sparks."

"Boxes?" said Remi, for he'd only seen the purple box.

Leo cringed – he'd spilled the beans.

"You found another box! That's awesome!" Remi

glanced around the lobby, searching for the hidden boxes. "They must be important, right? The first one's got Merganzer's head on it and everything. Wait a second . . . you said the purple box had duck food in it."

"I barely knew you back then," said Leo. "I had to come up with *something*. For all I knew, you were working for Ms Sparks."

"Are you kidding? She won't even give me a toilet break!"

But Remi wasn't hurt. He understood that it took at least six or seven hours to cultivate a trusting friendship.

"So what's in the boxes?" he asked.

Before Leo could answer, a voice, splashed with a rich Spanish accent, filled the lobby.

"Remilio? Time to go, sweetie."

"Mum! Please don't call me that. It's embarrassing."

"Leo?" Pilar said, finding them at the duck elevator. "You'd better head for the basement before Ms Sparks finds you. She needs some cooling-off time."

Leo couldn't help thinking Remi's mum was about to see the two boxes tucked beneath the rabbit bush, but it was Remi who spied them. Leo could see it in his round saucer eyes.

"And you, little hombre," said Pilar, putting an arm around her son. "We better get you home. You have a long day at the door tomorrow."

Remi groaned in agony at the thought of standing in the lobby with Ms Sparks all day, but he brightened when he remembered what his mother had told him.

"I'll show him around the place tomorrow afternoon," said Leo, reading Remi's thoughts. "I know the Whippet inside out."

Pilar was happy to see her son had made a friend in Leo, whom she had always adored. And Leo liked her, too. She'd covered for him with Ms Sparks lots of times.

"Skip the Cake Room, okay?" she said playfully, messing Remi's hair.

"You got it," said Leo.

"You guys can team up all you want." Remi smiled. "But if there's a Cake Room in this place, I'll find it."

Remi left with his mum and Leo grabbed the boxes, heading for the basement. When he came to the bottom step and creaked the door open slowly, he peeked inside, hoping not to see his dad drinking iced tea and reading *The New York Times*, old copies of which stood in three towering piles next to his bed.

"Dad, you in there?" Leo whispered. The basement wasn't huge, but it was very cluttered. Pipes, boxes, the call centre, the boiler, the washer, the clothesline and a lot more.

No one answered, so Leo crept inside, took the boxes apart and hid them under his bed, sighing with relief. At least the boxes were safely hidden, even if he was in trouble for going missing for several hours.

Leo heard the sound of the toilet flushing in the small bathroom off in the corner and realized he wasn't alone after all. He had a few seconds, though, which was just enough time to leave something on his dad's pillow.

"I thought I heard you come in," Leo's dad said. It was true Clarence Fillmore was a big guy, but he was more of a teddy bear than a growler. He didn't have it in him to scold Leo for disappearing.

"You know," he said as he sat down, "you're getting older now. If you need time to yourself, it's okay. Just let me know where you are, so I don't worry that you've fallen down the elevator shaft."

"Sorry, Dad," said Leo. "It won't happen again."

"And I got the ducks back to the roof for you. You know how Ms Sparks gets if we leave them in the grounds too long."

"Thanks, Dad."

Even at his young age, Leo knew his dad was a little bit broken, a little bit sad. There were reasons for this that Leo didn't like to think about, but one thing he knew for sure: he wouldn't lie to his dad, because he loved him too much. There would be no elaborate yarn about where he'd been that his father would probably believe.

"Good luck avoiding the wrath of Ms Sparks, though," Mr Fillmore said. "I can't save you from that."

Leo held his breath, waiting for his dad to see, wondering if he'd done the right thing.

"What's this?" the big man said, seeing the ring on his pillow and picking it up. The moment he did, Leo knew he'd made the right choice.

"I found it for you," said Leo, which was true.

Leo's dad didn't say anything. He stared at the ring as he lolled over and lay down on the sinking bed, moving it in the light.

"I don't know how you did it, but thank you."

They looked at each other then, smiling in a bittersweet sort of way. The ring had been missing a long time, but it was back now.

It had belonged to Leo's mother.

―――――――

Leo got up before daylight the next morning and went straight to the roof. He was too nervous to look inside the blue box with his dad snoring so nearby, but he knew by mid-morning the basement would be empty and he could safely investigate. Leo brought the ducks down and walked them through the lobby, all in a perfect line, out of the door and into the vast grounds. It was a short walk, partly because he knew Ms Sparks would soon arrive and he wanted to avoid seeing her, but also because Betty was in a foul mood.

"You miss Merganzer, don't you?" Leo asked, but she wouldn't look at him. Leo took the ducks safely back to the roof and returned to the basement, intent on starting his father's coffee brewing.

"How about we go to the big breakfast this morning?" Mr Fillmore said. "I have a feeling we're going to need it."

Leo began to protest, because it would mean seeing Ms Sparks. But then he reasoned that a) he could not avoid her for ever, b) breakfast at the Whippet was hard to resist and c) it was a good sign that his dad wanted to eat breakfast with everyone.

He'd been keeping to himself more and more, staying in the maintenance tunnels, avoiding contact with just about everyone.

Breakfast at the Whippet was brought over from the restaurant and served family style in the Puzzle Room, which was just off the lobby, across from the duck elevator. It was the one time when all the guests and staff members were invited to eat together. Often Leo was so busy during the day that he neglected lunch altogether and bolted down a late dinner, so the big breakfast was a must if he could get it.

"Leo Fillmore," said Ms Sparks as he stepped foot into the Puzzle Room. "Sit here, next to me."

Leo looked at Remi, who was ashen with concern for his friend, but there was nothing either one of them could do.

"Pass the hash browns," said LillyAnn Pompadore, and Leo sat down.

Ms Sparks was silent as Leo loaded his plate with eggs, bacon and blueberries. She had half a grapefruit and two vitamin pills, which struck Leo as one of the saddest things he'd ever seen, given the choices she had.

"You know, with Mr Whippet gone, I'm in charge," she said, only loud enough for Leo to hear as the guests and the staff talked and laughed.

"I do know that, yes," said Leo, trying to be as contrite as he could, for he knew this would please Ms Sparks.

"I could hire a new maintenance man. How would that be?"

Leo looked at Ms Sparks, frightened of what it would mean if they were tossed out on the street. He would never forgive himself if he got his father fired from the Whippet.

"Out with the old, in with the new. It has a certain ring to it, don't you think?"

Leo knew better than to grovel or make promises. Ms Sparks would not respond to such tactics. He took a bite of bacon, chewing quietly as her voice grew louder so everyone could hear.

"Mr Bump is having trouble with the robot again," she declared. "I want you up there the moment you finish that disgusting plate of food."

"Yes, ma'am," said Leo.

"And take him some breakfast."

Leo nodded.

Remi, who was in love with robots, piped in.

"You got robots up there?" he ventured, glugging down some milk as he waited for an answer.

"Yes," said Ms Sparks, staring at Pilar as she continued. "We *got* robots up there. Not that you'll be seeing them any time soon."

The accusing look seemed to indicate one of two things. Either Ms Sparks thought Pilar had done a poor job teaching her child English, or she was sending a veiled threat to the maid: *Don't let your little urchin out of the lobby while I'm gone, or else.*

Leo looked down the table and saw that everyone but Mr Bump and Mr Yancey had shown up. His dad was there, wearing the ring on a chain around his neck, which pleased Leo immensely. Ms Pompadore was holding Hiney, feeding him bits of sausage, and yacking with Mrs Yancey, the oil tycoon's wife. The bratty little girl, Jane Yancey, was downing powdered white doughnuts with frightening efficiency. And Mr Phipps stood with Captain Rickenbacker, drinking coffee and staring at the puzzle.

The puzzle was unusual for its size: there were eight hundred thousand pieces, which sat in pyramid-shaped piles on the longest table in the hotel (the length of twelve pool tables, to be exact).

"It's coming along nicely," said Captain Rickenbacker, gazing over the long table.

Mr Phipps didn't quite agree, as he stared at the

piles of pieces and the slight progress that had taken place in the years he'd been at the hotel, which were many.

"I would have hoped for better by now," he said. "But the edge does look nice."

He'd been the one to complete the edge of the puzzle, with Merganzer's help, about a year before, after which Merganzer had whispered a secret to the old gardener.

"There are two hundred and twenty-three ducks pictured in the puzzle. And a pond. And I'm in there, too." He had slapped Mr Phipps on the back, nearly knocking the black freckles off his old, dark face, and added, "That should get you moving in the right direction!"

Mr Phipps loved Merganzer, but he had no illusions about the puzzle. Clue or no clue, the puzzle would never be finished. It was just too big, too hard.

"Ducks, you say?" said Captain Rickenbacker, for Mr Phipps had let slip the secret.

"Ducks."

"Does this look like a duck?" asked the Captain, holding up a single yellow piece.

Mr Phipps said that he thought it did, then walked to the other end of the table, leaving Captain

Rickenbacker to hunt for pieces on his own.

"Why they waste their time on that ridiculous thing, I have no idea," said Ms Sparks, looking at the two men in disbelief.

"It's a Zen thing," said Clarence Fillmore. "Like meditation, or a rock garden."

"What on earth are you babbling about?" said Ms Sparks, who had no patience for mystical talk of any kind. She leaned over the table and turned her head to stare at Leo's father, her tall beehive hairdo precariously close to touching a pile of pancakes.

"I don't think finishing the puzzle is the idea," said Mr Fillmore.

Ms Sparks was clearly unimpressed. "I have a mind to take Pilar's vacuum to the whole mess and use the table for firewood."

The attention was off Leo, so he bolted from his chair, gathering a plate of baked goods for Mr Bump as he gave Remi a look that said *Keep your radio on, I'll be calling you.*

All Remi could think about was standing at the maddeningly dull door all morning, thinking about robots and cupcakes.

Afternoon couldn't come soon enough.

"Are you alone?"

The voice came from behind the door to Theodore Bump's room on the fourth floor.

"I am," said Leo.

"Hand me my breakfast," Mr Bump said, his arm sliding out from the cracked-open door. Leo put the plate in his hand, the door swung open a bit more and then the plate and the arm were gone. A moment later, the door flew open and Theodore Bump grabbed Leo by the arm, hauling him inside and slamming the door shut behind them.

"Can't be too careful, wouldn't you agree?" he asked Leo.

"I agree," said Leo. He had come to learn that more often than not in the Whippet Hotel, short and agreeable answers were safest.

The room was fabulous; there were no two ways about it. If it weren't for its eccentric guest, Theodore Bump, Leo would have liked to spend more time there. He was a kid after all, and all kids love robots.

Theodore Bump went to his desk and sat down, typing something out on a computer as he munched on a muffin. A familiar banging sound was coming from a room in the back, but Leo ignored it for the moment.

"I'm right in the middle of this, you understand? You'll have to deal with the problem yourself."

"Okay," said Leo.

He couldn't know if the rumours were true – no one knew. According to his father (and Pilar, who cleaned the room now and then), Mr Bump was a writer. That part wasn't so unusual. It was *what* he wrote, and how much, that made the rumours swirl. It was said that Theodore Bump wrote three novels a month under a total of nine assumed names. Pilar went so far as to say they weren't just *any* novels under *any* old names, but famous novels and famous names. To hear it from her, Mr Bump had written about half of the most popular books around.

Leo watched Mr Bump type at lightning speed for a moment more, then the man turned in his thread-bare blue dressing gown and stared at the boy, his grey hair matted on one side as if he'd got out of bed and gone straight to the keyboard.

"I don't like to be watched while I work. Do you mind?" he asked.

"Of course not," said Leo. When Theodore Bump turned back to the screen, Leo leaned in close behind him and tried to see what the man was writing. He thought he saw a wildly famous writer's name, but he couldn't be sure.

He left Theodore Bump and followed the banging sound at the other end of the room. The place was completely overrun with robots. Some of the robots were small and sat in clusters on tables and shelves. Others were eighty to ninety centimetres tall and stood on the floor with nothing whatsoever to do. Mr Bump had turned them all off because they made too much noise.

There were the bigger robots, some of them larger than Leo, and most of them with minds of their own. One made the bed, another vacuumed, another dusted all the other robots and one dispensed snacks. These Mr Bump allowed to work, so long as they didn't bother him. Merganzer had programmed them all himself, and he'd personally kept them in tip-top shape, visiting the Robot Room just about every day to check on them before he'd vanished.

Leo passed by a large, padded room, where the *really* big robots were kept. There were three – Klink, Klank, and Klunk – and all were over three metres tall. He was tempted to turn them on and watch them fight one another, which was highly entertaining. But it made an awful racket, and Theodore Bump would surely report Leo to Ms Sparks. Still, how could he see them standing there, heads bowed, silently staring at the floor, without turning them on? He promised himself he would return someday soon when Mr Bump was out for a walk and watch the robots rumble. Maybe he'd even bring Remi.

In Merganzer's absence, there was one particular robot that was causing Mr Bump a lot of problems. His name was Blop. Blop's job was "keeping company and making conversation", which meant he was pro-grammed to talk to guests in the room and make them feel at home. Unfortunately for Blop, Theodore Bump was *never* in the mood for conversation. In fact, Theodore Bump was so antisocial that it had begun frying Blop's circuitry. The more Theodore didn't talk to Blop, the more Blop felt he *needed* to talk. Sometimes he would go on and on and on about things no one wanted to talk about. He'd gone from being an interesting companion to an annoying chat-terbox.

Leo arrived at the door to the bathroom, the loud noise echoing inside. He opened the door and there was Blop, standing in the bathtub, banging his head over and over again on the porcelain. Blop was a small robot, about the size of a mug for hot chocolate. He was mostly silver, with large green eyes, and his metal mouth looked like it was made to eat coins.

When Blop saw that Leo had come into the bathroom, he rolled back and forth enthusiastically on his wheels.

"Mr Bump, is that you?"

"No, it's me, Leo."

Leo knelt down and laid his arms along the tub, setting his chin down on his hands as he stared at Blop. One thing was clear to Leo as he looked at the shiny silver robot in the tub: Mr Bump wasn't a violent man, for if he were, he would have picked Blop up and dropped him out of the window long ago.

"Oh, Blop," said Leo. "You really must stop bothering Mr Bump. You know how it upsets him."

"Very good to see you, sir," said Blop in his tiny, tinny voice. "You're looking excellent as usual. Tip-top."

The problem with Blop – besides the fact that he really *would not* stop talking – was that he was a sneaky little robot.

"Will you get me out of the tub?" he requested. "There's work to be done."

"You know he won't talk to you," said Leo. It was like trying to reason with an unreasonable child, he knew, but he had to try.

"He'll come round," said Blop. "I'm going to try Shakespeare."

"I could leave you in there and let your batteries run dry," Leo pointed out.

"Oh, you don't want to do that. My alarm will go off."

Merganzer had rigged Blop with a terrible alarm that would sound throughout the entire building if he got within five percent of a dead battery. It had only happened once, and Ms Sparks had nearly lost her marbles, screaming at everyone for days after. Even Merganzer had said it was something to be avoided at all costs.

"Besides," said Blop, "I'm solar-powered, as you know, and efficient. You'd have to leave me here in the tub for three days, two hours, twelve minutes and nine seconds in order to hear the alarm."

Blop started carrying on about solar power and alternative energy and how he and Merganzer had talked at length about putting wind turbines on the roof but that he worried for the ducks . . . and on and on, until Leo thought he might leave Blop where he was and shut the door.

Instead, Leo picked him up and placed him in his tool bag.

"Might I see Mr Bump now?" asked Blop. "I'd like to begin with the sonnets, which I believe he'll really enjoy."

Leo knew better than to engage Blop in conversation if he didn't need to. He kept walking until he reached the front door.

"I'll take him for a walk," he said to Mr Bump.

"Don't bring him back until Friday at least. Anything less would be a disappointment."

Theodore Bump didn't look up from his computer as he kept typing with one hand and held out the empty breakfast plate to Leo with the other.

Once in the hallway, Leo let Blop talk all he wanted. It would take all day to run him out of words, which was what Mr Bump had referred to. Blop preferred to say ten thousand words a day; after that he calmed down considerably. He would roll off into a corner and mumble quietly to himself, as if he were having robot dreams and talking softly in his sleep. Friday was three days away, so Leo would have to keep Blop talking for at least thirty thousand words.

He had an idea about how he could accomplish the task without having to carry the little robot around all day, and he was thinking about just that when his walkie-talkie came to life.

"Leo, get to the basement, pronto!"

It was his dad, who rarely sounded frantic about anything much lately.

"I see you have a Phillips screw driver," said Blop, who had burrowed his way right inside Leo's bag. And then he carried on about the origins of a great many tools as Leo ran down the maintenance stairs to the basement.

· CHAPTER 7 ·

TEN THOUSAND PAPER CLIPS

Leo found a cardboard box and a few old rags in the maintenance tunnel on the second floor on his way to the basement. He made a detour into the lobby to make a handover.

"You don't mean it," said Remi, staring into the box. "You *can't* mean it."

"Oh, but I do," said Leo. Blop was in the box, staring up at Remi with uncharacteristic silence.

"You're the best friend *ever*!" said Remi. Suddenly, standing next to a boring door all day didn't bother him. He had a robot, a *real* robot, to keep him company.

"Just keep him talking, and stay away from Ms

Sparks," Leo instructed. Ms Sparks knew the routine,

but it didn't make her any less annoyed by Blop's endless chatter. She'd only go for it if Remi kept the robot outside, like a pet that hadn't been house-trained.

"*Best* day in the history of my *life*!" said Remi. They were standing just outside the door together, where Remi had placed the cardboard box on the ledge of a window next to the entryway.

"Keep your radio on," said Leo, heading for the basement. "In case I need you."

"You got it, partner," said Remi.

Blop had begun yacking on about the meaning of friendship in all its facets, but the moment Remi said the word *partner*, the robot made a few noises – a *blip*, a *zing*, a *whir* – and looked at Remi.

"What do you think of Batman and Robin?"

Remi lit up like a sparkler.

"It asked me a question!"

Leo was already in the lobby, his two-way radio buzzing with demands, as he yelled over his shoulder.

"Get used to it."

When he entered the basement, Leo thought the police, the fire department and the county health inspector had all shown up at once. Every colour of light was spinning and flashing on the wall, the siren was going off and streams of red ticker tape were pouring out of Daisy's mouth like an endless supermarket receipt.

"Leo!" yelled Clarence Fillmore. "The hotel is sick!"

At first this struck Leo as an odd thing to say, but the more he looked at the call centre, the more he had to agree: the Whippet Hotel had come down with something really bad.

"What do we do?" Leo yelled over the blaring siren.

"We have to convince everyone to stop pulling their emergency cords," said Clarence Fillmore, shaking his head in disbelief. "I've never seen anything like it."

Every guest room had a red ball hanging from a red rope. On the wall near the ball was a red button. To send a distress signal, a guest had to grab the ball and pull the cord while simultaneously pressing the red button. The rope and the button were too far apart (and the rope too high) for a child to make trouble. Apparently, from the look of the call centre, all the guests in the hotel were pulling their cords and pressing the buttons in their rooms at the same time, over and over again.

All Leo could think about was how Ms Sparks would use this to try to fire his dad. She'd say it was his fault the hotel was falling apart.

"You take Ms Pompadore – you're good with her – and I'll take Captain Rickenbacker. Let's start there."

The first thing they had to do was get the siren to stop wailing, which would mean getting at least one guest to stop pulling on his cord.

The call centre had an old-fashioned-looking bank of buzzer buttons across the middle under Daisy's head. Clarence pushed the button for LillyAnn Pompadore's room and Leo for Captain Rickenbacker's, hoping they'd let go of their emergency cords long enough to answer the calls.

Mercifully, the siren stopped wailing in the basement boiler room as both guests picked up at once, their voices distant and crackly.

"The Pinball Machine has gone berserk!" yelled Captain Rickenbacker. "It's trying to kill me!"

"WET FLOOR, HINEY CAN'T SWIM!" was all Ms Pompadore would say, although she said it so loudly that both Fillmores leaned back as if a strong wind had blown into the basement.

"At least the siren stopped," said Leo, and the moment he said so, the siren began sounding again.

"You've jinxed us," said Leo's father, looking at the call centre lights flashing like mad.

Fifteen minutes later, Leo and Clarence Fillmore had everyone calmed down. The call centre was still blinking red, but at least they could quietly assess the damage.

- *Water leaks in at least three rooms, which Leo rightly blamed on a leak in the pond pump on the roof.*
- *Air conditioning not working in four rooms. It was only midmorning and already the temperature was over twenty-five. If it got above thirty-two in the Cake Room, they'd be looking at an icing disaster, very hard to clean up.*
- *Electrical shorts in the Pinball Machine and the Robot Room. Klink, Klank and Klunk were in a battle royal that threatened to drive Mr Bump out of the hotel and into a café with his laptop.*
- *There was no hot water in the hotel, which meant the boiler was on the blink.*

"Leaks first, then everything else," said Leo's dad, staring at the strips of ticker tape and wondering how they were ever going to get it all fixed.

Leo was just about to encourage his father – they'd work it out, he was sure – when the door to the basement opened and the shadow of Ms Sparks's towering beehive leaned into the room.

"You're on thin ice, Mr Fillmore. I hope, for your sake, you can get things under control around here."

"Absolutely, Ms Sparks. Leo and I are handling it. No need to worry."

"Why am I not consoled?" she said, looking at the Fillmores' bunks as if she couldn't imagine having to live in such primitive quarters. She slammed the door shut and Leo listened as her high-heeled shoes clanked up the concrete steps to the lobby.

"I'll fix the water pump, you mop up the rooms," said Clarence.

"Then I'll take the duck elevator to the maintenance tunnel on four and fix the electrical panel. It's the same panel for the robots and the Pinball Machine."

"Perfect! We'll meet back here in an hour to wrestle the boiler into shape."

Leo and Clarence loaded their tool belts and bags

with everything they could imagine needing, and then Leo called Pilar on the maintenance line and asked her to switch on the wet/dry vac system on all floors and bring out the mops.

The siren started wailing again as voices blared into the basement.

"Let's get out of here before she blows!" Clarence joked, and he and Leo were off, fixing things on every floor.

In all the excitement, Leo wasn't able to get his hands on the blue box, which just about drove him half crazy with anticipation. He knew it would lead him somewhere secret in the hotel, but he couldn't rightly go exploring while the Whippet was in the fight of its life. He'd never known the hotel to suffer so many calamities, but then again, Merganzer D Whippet was forever tinkering with every part of the building. A hundred and one days without him at work might have finally caught up to the quirkiest hotel in New York.

"Yo, Leo."

Remi was calling on the two-way radio as Leo entered the maintenance tunnel and started up one of the ladders towards the wet rooms.

"I'm kind of busy at the moment, Remi," Leo said,

trying to climb the ladder with one hand as he held the radio.

"Blop caught wind of the water leaks and he's worried about the other robots," Remi reported. "He keeps banging his head against the cardboard box."

Leo rolled his eyes. "He's a tricky robot; don't let him fool you. He's just trying to get back to the room so he can bother Mr Bump. Try talking about racing cars. He likes that."

"If you say so," said Remi. "He also taught me about hot-water heaters and hotel boiler rooms. He must have heard Ms Sparks talking about how nobody had hot water. This little guy is *clever*."

Leo wished Remi would leave him alone so he could concentrate on getting his work done.

"He said when the boiler stops sending hot water, it usually means it's about to blow a gasket. Wouldn't that be cool?"

A light went off in Leo's brain as he realized Blop might be right. The boiler might start to leak, a lot. The boiler was in the basement, and so was the blue box.

"Remi, listen carefully," said Leo, jumping off the ladder into the tunnel on seven. "I need you to do something for me, but it's going to mean leaving the front door. Can you do that?"

Leo walked down the tunnel to a hidden door that opened into the hotel hallway and headed for the maintenance cupboard, where Pilar would be waiting with the wet/dry vac.

"Yeah, I can help! Ms Sparks cancelled her errands, but now she's running around all over the place, so I'm sure I can sneak off. Apparently the hotel is falling apart. I'm the least of her problems."

"There are two boxes under my bed in the basement."

"The *secret* boxes," Remi said, with great emphasis on the word *secret*.

"Yeah, those." Leo couldn't help shaking his head. "Take the blue one and put it in the duck elevator for safe keeping. No one else goes in there."

"Me and the Blopster are on the prowl," said Remi. "Consider it done!"

Pilar was already pushing her maid's cart away from the cupboard when Leo rounded the corner.

"What's happening to the Whippet?" she asked, with concern in her dark brown eyes.

"I don't know. I guess it's sick," Leo answered.

"Or sad," said Pilar. "I think it misses Mr Whippet."

Leo didn't know about that, but there was no

getting around the fact that the hotel was in real trouble.

Leo headed for Ms Pompadore's room as the two-way radio flared to life again.

"She's gonna blow!" he heard Remi's voice scream, followed by Blop describing water survival techniques. "The giant black boiler is shaking and steaming – I think it might start blowing bolts and shooting water all over the basement at any moment! I have to get Blop out of here – it'll fry his circuits if he gets wet!"

Blop began to disagree, saying he was a fine swimmer, which was utter nonsense.

"Did you get the box?" Leo asked.

"Who are you talking to?" Ms Pompadore questioned, and Leo quickly turned the radio off, stuffing it in the pocket of his overalls. She looked at him as if he were hiding something.

"Just boring maintenance talk, Ms Pompadore. I should have this cleaned up in no time," he said, trying to change the subject as Hiney growled and begged to be put on the floor. There were only a couple of centimetres of water confined to the main bathroom, but Ms Pompadore wouldn't let the poor thing down. "It's a little funny, don't you think?"

asked Leo, trying to lighten the mood under Ms Pompadore's steady gaze. "I mean, this being the Room of Ponds and Caves and all."

"I fail to see the humour," she answered. "Water belongs in the sink, the toilet and the ponds. Not on my bathroom floor."

"Yes, ma'am," said Leo.

"I suppose next you'll be telling me I ought to have bats landing in my hair because there are caves in my room."

"No, ma'am," Leo said, although he did think that sounded kind of logical.

Ms Pompadore moved away and Hiney barked about a thousand times while Leo worked the wet/dry vac. He knew he should call his father and send him to the basement in case the boiler was pouring water all over their room, but Leo wanted to make sure Remi had safely moved the blue box first. He finished mopping up, put the wet/dry vac away, checked the fourth floor electrical panel and practically dived down the stairs on his way to the basement. Before he could get there, his dad radioed him.

"Better get back to the basement," Clarence Fillmore said. "There's something weird down here I need to talk to you about."

Uh-oh. Leo was sure his father had found Remi and the boxes, and his amazing adventure in the secret rooms of the hotel would be over for good. He tried calling Remi a whole lot of times but he got no answer. When he reached the door to the basement, he listened carefully, hoping not to hear the siren or flowing water.

"Hey, Dad," he said, entering the room. The boiler was in the darkest corner of the basement, set on a huge slab of concrete. There was a drain valve that let water flow out under the garden and into the sewer system, and Mr Fillmore was crouched down over the hole, watching water flow out.

There was no sign of the blue box. Only the purple one was there. Maybe his father hadn't found them after all.

"Come here," Leo's dad said. "You've gotta see this."

Leo slowly moved across the room, leaning down when he passed his bed in order to look underneath. It was too dark in the basement to tell for sure, but if he had to guess, he'd have said the blue box was gone.

"What is it, Dad?"

Mr Fillmore pointed a torch towards the flowing water, steam rising up from the heat. He pulled a thirty-centimetre-long magnetic tube out of his tool belt, which he used for picking up nuts and bolts that had fallen into out-of-the-way places, and held it down in the water.

"Are those . . . ?" asked Leo, but he didn't finish.

"Yup, paper clips. Tons of 'em."

The magnet was filling up with globs of metal paper clips as they poured out of the boiler.

"I bet there's ten thousand," said Mr Fillmore as they both listened to the paper clips grinding their way through the giant boiler.

"But how?" asked Leo.

Neither of them spoke for a long moment, because they both knew the truth. There was only one reason something like this would happen. And there was plenty of other evidence to support what they were both pretty sure of.

Someone was trying to sabotage the Whippet Hotel.

━━━━━━━━━━━━━━━━━

"That was our contact," said Milton, hanging up his phone. "They've set things in motion."

"And the competition? What of them?" asked Bernard. He seemed troubled. He'd been so sure of his control over the Whippet, but he was less sure with each passing day. His plans were moving along precisely as he'd hoped, and yet he doubted.

Milton looked gravely through the gate into the Whippet's sprawling grounds.

"We'll have to choose carefully if we hope to defeat our enemies."

"True," said Bernard Frescobaldi. "Take me back to the park. I want to take one last look around."

"Yes, sir."

Bernard had just read another highly confidential diary entry by Merganzer D Whippet, this one about Central Park, and he thought it best to go there at once to search for something he might have missed. So many clues, so much to remember. And so much at stake. He couldn't let the slightest clue slip through his fingers.

"Isn't the Central Park Room at the Whippet a wonder?" he asked, scanning the words once more. "Magnificent."

"Agreed," Milton said.

When they pulled to a stop on Central Park West, Bernard got out of the black town car and began walking alone. He brought the diary entry with him, and after a while sat down on a bench and read it once more.

Merganzer D Whippet, entry the nineteenth

Mother had an unexpected burst of energy one day. She took me to the Metropolitan Museum of Art because, she said, an artist was having a rare show. She was convinced I would be captivated. She could not have been more right.

Joseph Cornell made the most fantastic picture boxes I'd ever seen. I had loved art before, but this was different. My mind worked in 3-D, and seeing the picture boxes filled with trinkets and words and colours left me breathless. I knew then that I would make intricate boxes of my own some day.

She grew tired, but I wouldn't leave until I'd seen every one.

Afterwards she wanted fresh air, so we walked in Central Park, talking about Cornell and trains and robots and so much more. We stopped and sat beneath the spire of Belvedere Castle, eating from a bag of crispy doughnuts.

"Do you really love all these things?" I asked her, because I still held a deep suspicion that she talked about what I loved, not what she loved.

"I love *you*, Merganzer, and that's all that really matters."

I thought then, as I do now, that it was the most perfect answer of them all.

It was the last time we walked together, there in the park. After that she never left the apartment on Fifth Avenue.

MDW

CHAPTER 8

INTO THE PARK

After Remi had put the blue box in the duck elevator, he returned to the lobby just in time to open the door for Ms Sparks.

"PHIPPS!" she screamed, and Mr Phipps, a slow mover at best, began walking towards the lobby. He had a wobbly gait, which Blop began talking about in cryptic medical terms only a back surgeon could understand.

Ms Sparks gave the little robot an icy stare, though she knew it was hopeless. Short of throwing Blop across the lawn, there wasn't much she could do to shut him up.

". . . and so you see, walking is far more complex

than one might imagine at first glance. Wouldn't you agree?" asked Blop, looking at Ms Sparks hopefully, as if his only wish in the world were that she would answer him.

Instead she turned to the gardener as he arrived at the step.

"I need you to watch the front desk until I return," she demanded. "Something's come up."

It was a hot day, and Mr Phipps pulled out a handkerchief, mopping his brow. "If you insist."

Ms Sparks was not fond of sweat and made a sour face, but she needed to go and Pilar wouldn't be available until two o'clock. She looked at her wristwatch – noon – and scurried down the path towards the gate.

"I'll be back before the dinner bell at six. Pray the building doesn't fall over before I return!"

Remi and Mr Phipps watched her disappear down the winding path without a word. As soon as she was out of earshot, Mr Phipps turned to Remi.

"I'll be working on the puzzle. Don't get into any trouble."

"I can't get into trouble here at the door," said Remi. "Unless you count DYING of BOREDOM."

"Who said anything about standing by the door?"

said Mr Phipps. He was already inside, heading for the Puzzle Room without the slightest care about who might enter the building in the absence of a boy at the door or a gardener at the front desk.

Remi looked at Blop, who was staring up at him hopefully, and broke into a wide grin.

"Let's go see what's in the blue box."

―――――――

"What do you mean, you're on the fifth floor? I thought you were glued to the front door?"

Leo was standing before a jumble of wires at the electrical panel on floor six. The pipes were all painted different colours and they twisted and turned around one another, creating a spaghetti rainbow effect that made Leo's head spin. Add to that what looked like a thousand miles of wires dangling from the ceiling and it was a miracle the whole place didn't self-destruct from an overload of chaos. It was one of the more confusing places in the maintenance tunnel, and it required Leo's full attention to get anything done.

His concentration blown, Leo stepped back from the electrical panel and listened as Remi told him about Ms Sparks's early departure and his exploration of the blue box. When Leo understood what Remi had done, he felt angry. It was *his* box, not Remi's, and now Remi had opened it without him.

"I checked the register and no one has stayed in the Central Park Room since Mr Whippet disappeared," Remi reported. "What's in there?"

Leo didn't want to talk about the Central Park Room.

"It's not your box. You shouldn't have opened it."

"But you told me to go and get it," Remi pleaded, all the excitement gone out of his voice at the thought of upsetting Leo.

"I didn't tell you to open it. You shouldn't have done that."

"I was only trying to help."

Leo looked at the mess of wires and blown fuses before him and knew he couldn't possibly fix the air conditioning in less than half an hour. After that, he'd have a little time – maybe an hour – in which to disappear in the labyrinth of the hotel.

"It's okay," he said, trying to let go of something he really did think was his and his alone. "Just ask next time."

"Next time?" said Remi, his old zing returning. "You mean there are *more* boxes in this place? Awesome!"

"We're supposed to bring a duck," said Leo, thinking it would be the perfect errand for Remi and Blop while he finished the electrical work. "Go to the roof and get Betty – she's the smartest of the bunch. Then meet me at the door to the Central Park Room. We're going in."

"Yes!" cried Remi. "You hear that, Blop? We're going in!"

Leo went back to work on the wiring, pulling crystal fuses and electrical tape out of his maintenance bag. While Remi went up in the duck elevator, he told Leo what was inside the blue box.

"Trains and tracks, mostly," said Remi.

"Trains?"

"I know, weird, right? There isn't a train in Central Park, but it says right on the inside of the lid: 'Enter through Central Park on five, under the arrow.'"

"Have you been to Central Park before?" asked Leo. He had set the two-way radio on a ledge, pushing the button when he needed to while his hands worked quickly at the wires and fuses.

"Of course I've been to the park. Who hasn't?" said Remi. He asked Leo why Blop was being so quiet.

"If he blows through ten thousand words in under

an hour, it usually shuts his voice chip down for a little while. You must have had quite a chat this morning."

"Oh yeah, we talked about everything. He's my travel buddy."

Leo could imagine Remi in the small elevator, sitting on the floor with Blop on his lap in the cardboard box. The two boys were like secret spies making their way through a hidden world, not knowing what they'd find around the next corner.

"'Under the arrow,'" said Leo, running electrical tape around a bunch of red and yellow wires. "I don't know about any arrows in the park. We might have to do some searching to find the entrance."

"I'm at the roof," said Remi. "But Betty won't get in. She's in a bad mood. Should I bring a different duck?"

Leo thought about wandering through Central Park with a robot, a duck and a buddy, and he thought better of the idea.

"I think we can manage without Betty this time," said Leo, screwing in the last fuse and throwing the electrical switch. A whirling noise ensued, and Leo knew the air conditioning was back up again. He was a free man, at least until his dad found out he'd finished fixing the AC in record time. "Head back down and knock on the door. I'll open it from the inside."

"How're you gonna do *that*?"

Leo didn't answer. It was best if only he and his dad knew about some of the undisclosed ways into the rooms in the hotel. Merganzer had been clear about this when he'd hired Clarence Fillmore: some places were known only to the few, the proud, the maintenance men.

Leo called in on the Cake Room on six and knocked on the door, hoping no one would be in. His hopes were dashed when Jane Yancey answered. She had icing on her nose.

"Took you long enough," she said. Jane had attitude to spare as she bit into a cupcake and talked with her mouth full, spitting crumbs all over the floor. "We were *boiling* in here. My dad's going to get a refund."

"Can I come in and check a couple of things?" asked Leo.

Leo was surprised to hear Mr Yancey's voice from inside, sounding exasperated.

"Let him in, honey. The boy's got work to do."

Jane Yancey stepped aside begrudgingly, wiping

icing on her pink tank top. The room was cooling down fast as Leo entered, thinking about how he'd never actually seen Mr Yancey. The guy was like a ghost, normally off at some meeting. All he knew for sure was what Ms Sparks had told him: Mr Yancey was a zillionaire, into precious metals and oil reserves, and not to be bothered.

The room itself was breathtaking, full of huge models of wildly decorated cakes and sweets, which could be climbed and slid down and played on. Here and there were glass doors, behind which were rooms filled with real cakes and treats, all replaced by the restaurant staff every morning.

"Do you mind if I check the cold room?" Leo yelled towards the bedroom, hoping Mr Yancey would come out and introduce himself.

"Be my guest, but don't let Jane in there. She's had enough treats for one day."

Jane scowled as Leo stepped into the huge refrigerator. When he came back out, Mr Yancey was standing next to his daughter.

"Her mother's out shopping, spending all my money," he said. Leo was immediately struck by how dark the man's appearance was against the bright colours of the room: black suit, black hair, black shoes, a black coffee mug. He was a big man with a big face and a bald head. Leo could imagine him on an oil rig, barking out instructions, and wondered if that was where he'd got his start. Mr Yancey looked to Leo as though he belonged in dirty flannel shirts and thick work trousers smudged with black oil, drilling into hundreds of metres of earth, searching for treasure.

Leo had forgotten to turn off the two-way before entering the room, and to his horror, Remi's voice filled the Cake Room.

"Okay, Leo, where are you? Not funny. Blop is waking up."

"Hey, I know that voice," said Jane Yancey. "It's the stupid kid from the lobby. What's he doing? And who's Blop?"

Leo started for the door as Mr Yancey watched him curiously.

"Everything's tip-top," he said with a nervous smile. "But if you have any problems, you know how to find me."

Leo was out of the room before Jane Yancey could ask him any more questions, but she turned to her father, her arms folded over her chest.

"Those two are up to something."

Mr Yancey, for his part, sipped his black coffee and wondered how much Leo Fillmore really knew about the Whippet Hotel. He shrugged and went back to his room, saying over his shoulder, "Don't get into any trouble until your mother gets back."

But Jane Yancey had a better idea, and soon she was out of the door without Mr Yancey having a clue.

The fastest way down to the fifth floor was the main staircase, so Leo ran down it, nervous in case Jane Yancey chased after him. When he arrived at the door to the Central Park Room, Remi was gone.

"Oh, great, just what I need."

Leo didn't have a key card for the door, and it was a bit of a trick getting in through the maintenance tunnel from where he stood. He pulled out the radio just in time to hear Jane Yancey's voice from up the stairs.

"Maintenance man?" She had followed him, as he'd suspected she might, and it wouldn't take long for her to reach his floor and start asking all sorts of questions.

Without warning, the door to the Central Park Room flew open and Leo heard Blop's voice.

"Ah, Mr Fillmore, welcome to the park. We've been expecting you."

Leo darted inside and the door closed silently behind him. He didn't have to ask Remi how he'd got in, because Remi was holding a green key card in his hand. He'd made off with it while Ms Sparks was away and the front desk was unmanned.

Not bad, thought Leo. *Not bad at all.*

There came a knock at the door, Jane Yancey for sure, but the two boys ignored her pleas and began walking.

"I know you're in there! Let me in!" she screamed from the hall.

"She will prove troublesome," said Blop, rested and full of words again. "Very common for a six-year-old, particularly if you spoil them."

Leo saw that Remi had brought the blue box with him, carrying Blop in the pocket of his red jacket, from where the robot peeked out inquisitively.

"One good turn deserves another," said Leo, thinking of how Remi's key card had got them into the room. Opening up his maintenance bag, Leo pulled out a squashed cupcake, which he had snuck out of the refrigerator in the Cake Room.

"Nice!" said Remi, setting the blue box down and

sliding off the lid. He broke the treat in half as they settled over the box and gazed inside.

"This Merganzer guy was a little wacky," said Remi, handing half the cupcake to Leo. Both boys were starving, and the cupcake vanished in one bite each.

"You have no idea," Leo tried to say, but it came out *oo av oh ieeaa* as he tried to speak through a mouthful of cake. Remi thought it was hilarious and started laughing, then rolling around on the floor in hysterics. Leo joined in and they were both sharing a good laugh, which unfortunately Jane Yancey could hear from the other side of the door. She marched away, determined to ruin their lives or die trying.

When Leo and Remi calmed down, they looked inside the box and found that it was filled with the most intricate model train set either of them had ever seen. There were rolling hills, tunnels, trees and a farm. The train engine itself was the size of Leo's thumb, with two silver carriages behind it.

"Watch this," said Remi. He reached inside and pushed a tiny lever forwards and the train started to move. Leo wished he'd been the one to see this first, but watching the miniature train make its way around the box was so magical, he could hardly stay angry.

"What does it mean?" Remi asked as the train continued round and round.

"There's only one way to find out," said Leo, standing up and looking out over the Central Park Room. "We'll have to find the train and climb aboard."

Remi smiled, icing in his teeth, and the two boys started laughing again. Then they started walking.

An arrow was hidden somewhere in the Central Park Room, and it wouldn't be easy to find.

CHAPTER 9

THE CENTRAL PARK TRAIN

"I love this hotel," said Remi. He and Leo were standing in front of Balto, a statue of a dog staring out over the rest of the room. The real Central Park sat on 843 acres in Manhattan, but Merganzer had crammed every last attraction into one floor of the Whippet. For that reason, Balto was only about five centimetres tall. As the boys leaned in and looked more closely, Blop regaled them with the story of the extraordinary sled dog.

"If you'd have told me when I woke up this morning I'd be standing in a shrunken Central Park listening to a robot tell me about a five-centimetre-high dog," said Remi, "I'd have said you were nuts.

How in the world did anyone ever build this?"

"You haven't seen anything yet," said Leo, thinking of the Room of Rings, the Pinball Machine, the Cake Room and so much more that Remi hadn't seen yet.

"I believe you," said Remi. "From what my mum told me, the rooms get weirder, the higher you go."

Leo didn't want to spoil the fun and give too much away, but Remi was right. The seventh, eighth and ninth floors were bizarre, to say the least.

"Let's keep walking, see if we can find that arrow."

The winding path the two boys were on was sunk into the floor so that the model lay all around them at belly-button level. They could reach out and touch whatever they wanted, and Leo imagined Merganzer doing just that. He could see his old friend placing a tree here, a statue there.

Real water flowed under arched bridges, and the Lake was strewn with tiny boats and wobbling ducks. There were fountains, the Great Lawn, the Central Park Zoo, skating rinks, a carousel, baseball fields and tennis courts. Leo stopped in front of the statue of Alice in Wonderland, thinking he might have seen an arrow, but he was mistaken.

"Is it just me, or is it getting dark in here?" asked Remi.

"My sensors say yes, undoubtedly," said Blop. "Switching to reserve power."

As if there were a quickly moving sunset, the room was growing dim as they approached Belvedere Castle.

"Look there, it's a boy and his mum," said Remi. "The only two people in the park, right?"

"It's Merganzer," said Leo. "And that must be his mum." He could tell by the wild hair they both had, the way it flipped up at the back and looked like the feathers on the head of a merganser (the duck, not the person).

Stars filled the ceiling and the castle lit up as the room went completely dark. A moon appeared, bright and round, and shadows filled the room. The lights on the baseball fields came on, hundreds of tiny lamp posts glowed yellow and the sound of a distant train filled the room.

"Where's it coming from?" asked Remi. The sound was everywhere and nowhere at once. But Leo had grabbed Remi by the shoulder, staring off into the dark with fear in his eyes.

"Someone's in here with us," he said. In the

darkest corner of the room, a shadow worked the controls, changing the lights, making the moon come up.

"Who are you?" asked Leo. He was too afraid to move, but he began to wonder if they'd found Merganzer hiding in the Central Park Room.

The train whistle blew and Leo jumped. Lights began to dance on the Great Lawn, spinning and circling like fireflies.

"What's happening, Leo?" asked Remi. He was an adventurous boy, but this was getting scary.

"He's trying to help us," said Leo.

"Who's trying to help us?"

"I don't know, but look."

The lights on the Great Lawn had started to settle, gathering together to form words. Leo and Remi read them silently, and when they did, the words burst into tiny flames and the room was light once more.

The sound of the train was gone, and so was the shadow.

Leo said the words to Remi. *"Every arrow needs a bow."*

Both boys had been to Central Park enough times to know what it meant right away. It had to be Bow

Bridge, the most famous bridge in the park, which stretched across the Lake.

Blop went full throttle about all the bridges in the park, for there were many, and for once Remi wished he could get the robot to be quiet. It was no time for detailed information about why they used cast iron to build bridges in the park and how the Bow Bridge, built in 1862, had been photographed about a billion times.

"If you put him face down, he's harder to hear," said Leo. Remi picked Blop out of his jacket pocket and turned him upside down, dropping him back inside. His wheels spun back and forth with a *whir*, but his muffled tin voice dropped into the background.

When they arrived at the Bow Bridge, Leo was the first to spot the hidden arrow. Under the arch, near the water, a cluster of ducks was staring.

"There it is," said Leo.

"It makes me wonder if there's an arrow under the real bridge," Remi pondered. "I'll have to get a boat and see next time I go there."

Leo smiled at this idea, because he'd been thinking the same thing. Maybe the two of them could go together once all the mysteries of the hotel had been solved.

Leo reached over the grass and the trees and took hold of the gold-plated arrow, which was about the size of a toothpick. He pulled and nothing happened.

"Try pushing it in," said Remi, who was impatient by nature.

Leo tried and, again, nothing happened.

"Let me have a try," said Remi, reaching past Leo to grab the little arrow.

"No, I can do it," Leo said. He'd missed opening the blue box and he wasn't about to let Remi open a secret room in *his* hotel.

Leo and Remi both reached for the arrow at once, but Remi got there first. Leo, in his frustration, tried to push Remi's hand aside. When he did, the arrow snapped off in Remi's hand.

"Now look what you've done!" said Leo.

Remi had always been a daring, energetic boy, but he was also tender-hearted, his confidence easily shaken.

"I'm sorry, Leo. I didn't mean for that to happen. I just got so excited."

Leo turned back to the Bow Bridge, his frustration made worse by the fact that Remi didn't fight back. Remi turned to Blop for comfort, pulling him out of his red jacket pocket and asking him for help.

"Blop, how do we find the train?"

Blop's head spun back and forth as he scanned the park, the Lake, the bridge. He seemed to be thinking.

"The ducks have turned, which is very odd indeed. Might that be of interest?"

Leo, a glimmer of hope returning, moved in close to the ducks. It was true; they had all turned, their miniature heads now facing the other side of the bridge.

"Remi," said Leo. "Give me the arrow."

Remi handed the toothpick-size arrow, the tip of which had been broken off, to Leo. He leaned in, too, and saw what Leo saw.

"A bull's-eye! No way!" Remi yelled. He was so excited, in part because he realized the arrow was *meant* to be broken off, but even more because the rupture between him and Leo had been repaired. All was not lost after all!

Leo stuck the arrow in the centre of the bull's-eye and stepped back as a hole opened up in the ceiling over their heads.

"Better move back – I've seen this happen before," warned Leo.

Remi was a perceptive listener, and as the ladder shot down out of the ceiling, he thought he heard something else from the other end of the room.

"So cool!" he said, because it was, and then he added, "I think someone might be trying to get in here."

Leo stayed very still and listened. Someone was fumbling with a key card in the hall, trying to get the door open. Leo looked at Remi and put a finger to his lips, then he started up the ladder as fast as he could go.

———

When Jane Yancey finally got the key to work, she opened the door to the room only a crack, hoping she would catch Leo doing something he shouldn't be doing, and be able to turn him in. She thought she heard a swishing noise, but she couldn't be sure. The room had turned completely dark, and she opened the door wide, proud of herself for sneaking downstairs and making off with the key while no one was in the lobby. *I'm a crafty girl*, she thought to herself. She let the door go as she searched for a light switch, not realizing the door was on a spring, and it slammed behind her.

She felt she was not alone.

"Hey, Maintenance Man! You get out here right now! Stop trying to scare me!" she screamed, but now she wasn't so sure. Maybe the maintenance man hadn't entered this room. Maybe she should get out, fast, and never come back.

Jane Yancey got hold of the handle and threw the door open, afraid to look over her shoulder and see someone chasing her.

She couldn't be sure, but as she ran down the hall, Jane thought she heard the sound of a distant train.

———————

"Oh no," said Remi. "I've done it again."

"Done what?" Leo asked. Neither of them had made it up the ladder before it shot back up into the hole, taking them with it. The hole had closed and they were in Merganzer D Whippet's secret Railway Room.

Remi wouldn't say, and Leo began to feel as if he'd made a mistake being so upset about the arrow.

"It's okay, Remi. You were right. I shouldn't have got so angry about the arrow. I'm sorry."

Remi seemed to perk up as he looked at the train waiting to be boarded. They were standing on a platform, the train was marked with a number 5, steam pouring out from under its wheels as though it wanted to go but wouldn't leave without them.

"I left the blue box behind," said Remi, wincing at the sound of his own words.

"Oh," said Leo. "That *is* bad."

"I know, I know – I blew it. I should never have put it down. Someone else might find the box, and then what will we do?"

But Leo was worried about something else entirely. Without the box they didn't have the model, which meant they'd have to work out how to get out of the room themselves.

"I didn't get a very good look inside," said Leo, trying to put a brave face on things. "Do you remember anything that might help us?"

"Not really. I mean, it was a train. There were lots of tracks and tunnels."

Not helpful, thought Leo. He was beginning to think inviting Remi into things had been a mistake, but then Remi had an awfully good idea. He pulled Blop out of his pocket.

"Blop, this is important, okay?"

"Important, yes. What is it?"

"Did you get a good look inside the blue box?"

Leo and Remi held their breaths as Blop's little

head turned back and forth between the two. Clearly the robot wanted to please Leo and Remi. He didn't want to let them down, and they were happy to find that he did not.

"It's the doughnuts you want, that's the trick," said Blop.

"What do you mean? What doughnuts?" asked Leo.

Blop's head twisted around and faced the train.

"Climb aboard and I'll show you."

Leo scratched his head and looked at the train. It was small, more like a roller coaster, and looking around the room he saw that the course it would take was filled with banks and sharp turns, ups and downs, tunnels and bridges.

"Wow, thanks, Blop! You totally saved us!" said Remi. Turning to Leo, he added, "Which car do you want?"

Leo wasn't sure they could trust Blop, but he wanted to, and he was glad Remi was the courageous type. He'd have hated to drag an unwilling participant on to a train bound for who-knew-where.

"I'll take the back carriage, you take the front," said Leo.

"You got it," Remi answered, setting Blop in his jacket pocket and climbing over the rail into the train carriage. Leo jumped into the last carriage and had a feeling of déjà vu. There was something familiar about the inside of the box he sat in, but he couldn't quite place it. There wasn't time to give it much thought, because the engine on the train began to lurch forwards on the tracks. When it did, Leo spied the seat belt in his train carriage and the light went off. He knew this carriage, and so he knew he'd better speak up.

"Put on your seat belt, Remi! You're going to need it!"

The engine was taller than the two carriages behind it, with a small round window in the back. Leo and Remi were sitting in the open air, and it was Remi who realized something first.

"Leo?" he said, as the train pulled out of the station.

"What is it?"

"Someone is driving this train."

Leo's heart raced as he looked past Remi and saw the round window in the engine car. It had fogged up, like the frosted glass in the Room of Rings, and someone was writing a message with their finger.

Hang on.

Leo's knuckles went white against the sides of the carriage as his grip tightened, and then the train shot out of the station so fast, it felt as if Leo's face had been blown off.

Remi howled with laughter, his jet-black hair fluttering in the wind as the train rounded the first tight turn and flew over a bridge. It was a rough ride, both boys being hurled back and forth in their carriages as they entered the first of three dark tunnels. Before they knew it, they were coming back into the station, which pleased Leo, because he expected the train to stop so they could get off.

This was not to be.

After the third time around, Leo and Remi both began to realize they weren't getting off the train unless they worked out what in the world they were supposed to do. It crossed Leo's mind that they might *never* get off the train.

"I'm going to hold Blop up in the air!" yelled Remi. He'd turned back to Leo, grinning from ear to ear.

"What? Why?!" Leo fired back.

Remi didn't answer as he spun back around, pulled Blop out of his pocket and held the small robot over his head.

"Don't drop him!" Leo said, half expecting Blop to

catch in the wind and nail him in the forehead as he flew by.

Around and around they went, no one speaking, all three of them watching. It was a surprisingly quiet and smooth ride, like a roller coaster on rails of jelly, and both boys took note of the route: two bridges, three wild turns, four ups and downs, three dark tunnels.

"Have either of you ever ridden a carousel?" Blop asked as they rounded a corner.

Leo and Remi both answered yes.

"So you've grabbed the dragon rings, then?" asked Blop. Remi didn't know what this meant, so he looked at Leo, who shrugged.

Up and down, over a bridge, and through a tunnel they went, rounding the station for the fourth time.

"Many carousels have the dragon ring feature," Blop continued, "which works like this: as you pass the dragon, you take the ring out of his mouth by hooking it with your finger. Every time a ring is taken, a new one appears. Take the gold ring and you get a free ride."

"Sounds fun, but what's it got to do with the train we're on?" Leo asked.

"The dragons are in the tunnels, or so says the blue box," said Blop.

Remi howled with delight, very happy that he'd given Blop a good long look inside the blue box. Even Remi hadn't seen the tiny dragon heads in the tunnels.

"Here comes a tunnel now!" Remi yelled, dropping Blop into his jacket pocket and leaning out of the car as the world went dark.

But it was useless. The tunnels were so dimly lit, they couldn't see anything – at least not until Leo took his torch out of his pocket.

"I'll point the light," he yelled. "You grab the rings!"

When they came to the second tunnel, Leo shone the light on the walls and there it was – a magnificent dragon head, its mouth open, a ring hanging from its teeth. Remi took off his seat belt and leaned far out of the carriage, so far that he nearly tumbled on to the tracks. His finger caught the ring and it popped free. There was a short pause as the train went by, then the dragon breathed a stream of fire, lighting up the tunnel with an orange glow. Leo had to duck below the flame in order to avoid having his hair set on fire.

"It's white!" Remi said.

"If Blop is right, we'll need a gold ring," Leo answered.

Around and around they went, collecting rings from the fire-breathing dragons, one in each tunnel. Every time a ring was taken, a new one appeared, until Remi had nine rings in his pocket. Through the station, up and down, over the bridge, and heading into the first tunnel – this time the ring was gold, as they'd both hoped.

"That's the one you want," said Blop, gazing out from his perch in the red jacket. "The gold ring is always the winner."

"Don't miss it!" said Leo, worried that the entire system would reset and they'd need to start all over again. He was starting to feel sick from all the times around the track and wanted to get off the ride more than ever.

Remi leaned out as they entered the darkness, Leo's torch guiding the way, the gold ring within his reach. But this time, he leaned too far.

"Remi!" yelled Leo.

Pointing the torch at Remi's carriage, he saw his friend dangling along the tracks as they flew by. The only thing holding Remi and Blop in the carriage was Remi's tennis shoe, which had caught on the door. They exited the first tunnel as Remi's red jacket flapped in the wind and he tried, without success, to grab hold of the carriage door. All nine rings flew out of his pocket, bouncing along the tracks behind them.

"Take my hand!" Leo yelled, unbuckling his seat belt and holding out his arm. A sharp right turn was seconds away, and Leo knew if he didn't get Remi in time, his shoe would come loose and Remi and Blop would go flying into the trees.

"Come on! Grab my hand! Now, Remi!"

Remi held his hands over his head just as they entered the turn and the shoe came unhooked from the train carriage. Leo had Remi by the hands, and as they rounded the sharp turn, he was nearly pulled out of his own carriage. Remi flew wide through the air, like a trapeze artist holding on to a partner. When the track turned straight again, Leo pulled hard and Remi tumbled into the second carriage, knocking Leo on to the floor.

"I lost it!" yelled Remi, pulling Leo up on to the seat by his overalls. "I lost the gold ring!"

But Remi needn't have worried, because the gold ring was safely held in Leo's hand.

"I have it," he said. It was big, about as wide

around as a billiard ball, and Remi thought it looked like a ring fit for a giant. There was a string attached to the ring, and attached to the string was an envelope the size of a postage stamp.

The train was nearing the second tunnel, and as it did, both boys saw flames.

"You've got to be kidding me," said Leo. The dragon in the second tunnel was breathing a steady stream of fire that filled the darkness. Without warning, the two carriages began to tilt backwards, until they locked into place with Leo and Remi lying flat on their backs, staring at the ceiling of the Railway Room.

"What's happening?" Remi asked, looking to Leo for help.

"No time for seat belts; just hold on as tight as you can!"

When the train engine neared the tunnel, it cut the carriages loose, racing through the fire all by itself. A hole opened in the floor, but Leo and Remi couldn't see it.

"Double Helix time!" yelled Leo.

"What do you mean, Double Helix time?" Remi yelled back.

The two carriages dropped into the hole, missing

the dragon flames by centimetres, and careered down the centre of the hotel.

"Awesooooooooooooome!" Remi howled, for he'd never been on the Double Helix before.

"I knew I recognized these carriages," Leo said, trying his best to hold on as the Double Helix spun them down five stories. Or was it six? The Double Helix lurched to a stop and Remi banged his head on the padded rail.

"Are you okay?" Leo asked worriedly.

"Are you *kidding*? Best hour of my life!" said Remi. He looked around the dark space and added, with grave concern, "Where's Blop?"

Both boys checked the jacket and the floor of the carriage, but Blop was nowhere to be found.

"He must have flown out of your pocket in the Railway Room," Leo said.

Remi looked like his dog had run away, his cat had been hit by a car, and his mother had grounded him for a week.

"What if he's smashed to pieces? What if we never find him?"

Leo was worried, but in a way, he was a little bit relieved to have left Blop in the Railway Room. Merganzer D Whippet built things tough, and Leo was sure Blop was rolling around, talking to the trees and the bushes and the grass.

"Don't worry. Blop is a very sturdy robot. We'll find him."

Remi brightened just a little. "You think?"

Leo put a hand on his buddy's shoulder. "Trust me, we'll find him."

Remi took a deep breath, nodded a couple of times, and seemed to regain some of the excitement he'd lost.

"I've never known the Double Helix to stop below ground," Leo said, glancing from side to side. "I think we're *under* the Whippet."

Both boys got out and stood next to the carriage, looking up into the tunnel they'd just fallen through. They were standing at the bottom of the shaft, where a ladder led up to a metal-grated landing.

"That's the lobby right there," Leo said, pointing up. "But we're three metres below that."

Leo scratched his head and looked at the gold ring. He noticed the postage-stamp-sized note tied with a string, and he was just about to take a closer look when Remi whispered.

"There it is."

"There's what?"

Leo followed Remi's gaze into the corner of the shaft. It was the same size as the others, but this one was bright green.

They'd lost a robot, but they'd found the third hidden box.

CHAPTER 10

THE FIELD OF WACKY INVENTIONS

No matter how hard they pulled on the wooden cover, Leo and Remi could not get the green box open. They were afraid of breaking whatever was inside, so rather than smash it against the wall, they carried it up the metal ladder. Leo went first, holding the box, and Remi followed, which was how Remi saw the message first.

"Something's written on the bottom."

When they reached the landing, Leo lifted the box over his head and read the words.

I won't open all alone.

"What do you think it means?" asked Remi, feeling in his jacket pocket and wishing, badly, that Blop were hiding there.

"Maybe if we slide all three boxes together, this one will open," said Leo.

"That's a great idea!"

They opened the orange door that led back into the lobby, but only a little, and saw Remi's mum sitting at the front desk. Leo left the green box behind and they crept out, bruised and battered, then shut the orange door behind them a little too loudly.

Remi's mum turned in their direction and tilted her head, staring curiously at the two boys.

"Ms Sparks isn't back yet?" asked Remi, trying his best both to distract his mum and to act as if nothing very exciting had happened in the past hour.

Pilar looked at her dishevelled son and wondered why his hair was standing up wildly on top of his head.

"Leo, are you keeping my boy safe? I hope you're staying out of trouble."

"Oh yes, ma'am. *Very* safe," said Leo, thinking as he said it that he'd almost allowed Remi to fall out of a moving train.

"I'd like to ride that thing sometime," said Pilar,

staring at the closed orange door. There was no hiding the fact that Leo and Remi had just ridden the Double Helix, but she didn't seem to mind, switching to a different topic. "Jane Yancey says you tried to scare her. Is that true?"

Remi jumped in. "She just wants to follow us around and bug us to death," he said. "You know how spoilt she is."

Pilar put her finger to her lips and looked across the lobby towards the Puzzle Room. "Mr Phipps is in there with Captain Rickenbacker. You know how he can be."

Leo knew, all too well, that Captain Rickenbacker was a terrible gossip who loved to entertain himself by stirring up trouble. If he'd heard them, he'd surely tell Mr Yancey what they thought of his daughter for the pure pleasure of seeing the sparks fly.

"Shoo," said Pilar. "MsSparks will be back at five o'clock sharp. I want you back at that door before she gets here."

Remi nodded his agreement and hurried off with Leo, glancing back at the door to the Double Helix and wishing they didn't have to leave the green box behind.

"It's a very small letter," said Remi. "We're going to need a magnifying glass."

They had arrived in the empty basement and opened the tiny envelope tied to the gold dragon ring.

"I've got just the thing," said Leo, going to one of the many toolboxes in the basement in search of a lens that had once been part of a pair of reading glasses. Mr Phipps had bought the glasses at a pound shop, thinking they might help his reading, but they'd only given him headaches, so he'd passed them on to Leo.

As Leo passed by the call centre, he saw a note left by his father with a list of jobs to do.

LEO,

THINGS STILL FALLING APART FASTER THAN I CAN FIX THEM! CAN'T HAIL YOU ON THE WALKIE-TALKIE (REMIND ME TO FIX THAT). FIND ME IN THE MAINTENANCE TUNNEL ON FOUR IF YOU NEED ME, OTHER- WISE HEAD UP TO SEVEN TO SEE MS POMPADORE AS SOON AS YOU CAN. TROUBLE WITH THE FISH.

DAD

PS. CHECK ON BETTY. SHE'S ACTING ODD.

"What's it say?" asked Remi. Leo had carried the note back with him to where Remi sat on the bed. "I've got some work to do, and it sounds like Betty might need another walk."

Remi didn't seem to mind. "I can walk the ducks if you need me to. I just wish we could get our hands on those boxes."

It was true; they were losing boxes almost as fast as they were finding them. The purple box was tucked safely under Leo's bed, but the blue one was in the Central Park Room, and the green one, which they hadn't even opened yet, was sitting in the first carriage of the Double Helix, which gave Leo an idea.

"I'll tell you what we'll do," he said. "I need to check in with Dad and fix the trouble on seven. That shouldn't take more than an hour. We'll tell your mum we need to get to the roof and fast or Betty and the rest of the ducks will revolt—"

"I see where you're going," Remi interrupted. "We'll get the green box on the way up, then split up on the way down in the duck elevator."

"You walk the ducks, I'll finish my work, then we meet in the Central Park Room—"

"—where we'll find the blue box and rescue Blop from the Railway Room!"

Leo hadn't thought about the part that included rescuing the robot, but they could cross that bridge when they came to it. Remi gave him the note that was in the envelope attached to the gold dragon ring, and the two boys leaned in close over the makeshift magnifying glass.

"How could anyone write so small?" asked Remi, but he was beginning to understand that a great many strange things could be found in the Whippet Hotel.

"That's odd," said Leo. "No one has stayed in that room for years."

"What's odd? What does the note say?"

Leo put his eye to the glass and read the note aloud.

" 'You are cordially invited to a dinner party on eight. Arrive 8 p.m. sharp. Do not be late! Mr M.' "

"It has to be Merganzer! He's here," said Remi. "He's come back."

But Leo wasn't so sure. There had been clues, but could it *really* be him, moving around in the hotel, secretly setting things in motion? He added things up in his head:

- *There had been someone in the Room of Rings or the Ring of Rooms.*

- *Captain Rickenbacker had been sure of seeing his imaginary arch-nemesis, Mr M.*
- *A dark figure had appeared in the Central Park Room.*
- *Someone had set the train in motion.*

And now this: a very tiny invitation to a dinner party on the only haunted floor of the hotel. It was all quite mad, really, but more than that, there was something about the whole business that didn't feel like Merganzer D Whippet at all.

"I think there's something else going on here," Leo said, stepping to the call centre to make a red Double Helix key card. "And I think you and I are going to get to the bottom of it."

"I'm with you," Remi said, standing up and putting the gold dragon ring in his jacket pocket. "Just tell me one thing. What's on the eighth floor?"

Leo handed Remi the red key card and started for the door.

"It's the Haunted Room. Didn't you know?"

Remi's face went pale. He hated ghosts and ghouls of any kind.

"No one's stayed on the eighth floor since I came here with my dad five years ago."

"Perfect," said Remi, but he was feeling better. As they came out of the basement, he could see the orange door that led to the Double Helix. He knew he was about to fly up the middle of the hotel.

Now *that* was the kind of thrill he liked.

The trouble with putting ponds in a hotel room is that they require constant care. Merganzer D Whippet had long visited the ponds daily in order to keep everything just so, but he'd been gone a hundred and one days and counting, which was a long time when it came to ponds. Not only had Leo been put in charge of walking the ducks every day in Merganzer's absence, he'd also been given the task of keeping the ponds in working order. He had, in the past few days, done a poor job.

It was for this reason that Leo had not been surprised to see the note from his dad: *Trouble with the fish*. Ms Pompadore had been staying in the Room of Ponds and Caves since her arrival. It had long been one of the most popular and expensive rooms, and Leo had to admit, it was a magnificent place to spend an afternoon.

"You see why I called," said Ms Pompadore, holding Hiney in one arm and a drink with a tiny umbrella in the other. There were seven ponds, all of which were shooting water from broken valves or pipes.

"Yes, ma'am," said Leo. "I can see why you called."

Leo had with him his pond tools: a retractable net, a hose with a latch that would let in fresh water from the maintenance tunnel, and a vest from which hung all sorts of wrenches, picks and hammers.

"I'm going into the theatre," said Ms Pompadore. "Come see me when you've finished and I'll have a tip for you."

Leo had to work not to roll his eyes, because Ms Pompadore's idea of a tip was usually in the range of a two-pence piece and a fluff-covered fruit gum.

Ms Pompadore set Hiney down, and the dog began to bark and run around the biggest of the seven ponds. Leo took a long look around, breathing in the deep green air as a blue dragonfly flew past. Paths wound all about the seven ponds in the room and wooden bridges crossed over the tops of each pool, from which a guest could look down on the lily pads, the jumping frogs and the colourful fish. The walls of the room were made of jagged black stone, where three large openings appeared. One led into the bedroom, another into a sunken pool and spa and the last into a theatre cave where guests could watch reality television or movies.

"Move aside, Leroy, and I mean it," said Leo. All the ponds were full of giant fish called koi, and Leroy was the biggest of the bunch. In the time that Merganzer had been gone, Leroy had got downright scary – over a metre long and fatter than a king-size watermelon. The only way he would let you pass without spitting water in your face was if you fed him boiled sweets, which Leo did. He tossed a handful of sweets to one side and Leroy swam lazily away.

When Leo arrived at the pump, he found that it was blocked, one of the medium-sized fish having got close enough to be sucked inside. Its tail was still wagging, a good sign, but getting it out would be impossible without the hose.

Leo moved a rock on the edge of the pond and found a plastic pipe, which he jammed the hose into. Then he turned it on full blast and the fish burst out of the pump and out of the water. If there were such a thing as a screaming fish, this fish would qualify. Hiney watched the fish spin through the air and belly-flop into the pond, and started barking all over again. Leo fed Leroy another handful of sweets and inspected one of the green plastic pipes, which was spewing water all over one of the paths like a broken sprinkler. He'd need to turn off the water and wrap the pipe in a special kind of tape that Merganzer had given him.

It took almost another hour to fix all seven ponds, and somewhere along the way Leo began to wonder about such a large number of problems. Pipes were known to crack, but this was ridiculous. All seven ponds at once?

"I've finished," said Leo, peeking into the theatre cave when at last he'd fixed every pipe. Ms Pompadore sat on a giant couch, watching a show that appeared to be about training dogs. This struck Leo as ironic, since Hiney was the least obedient dog he'd ever seen in his life.

"Be a doll and come back again tomorrow," said Ms Pompadore, her eyes never leaving the big-screen TV. "Those pipes are breaking by the hour."

"You should stop feeding Leroy," said Leo, feeling terrible for having fed the giant fish himself. "He's getting too big."

Ms Pompadore ignored Leo for a moment, then shook her eyeballs free of the TV.

"Did you say something?"

Leo shook his own head, hoping not to get into a long conversation with a bored Texas socialite.

"I've left a loaf of pumpernickel on the table for Leroy," she said, turning back to the show. "Be a dear and feed him on your way out. But don't give any to Hiney – he's on a diet."

Leo's eyebrows went up as he turned and started for the door. No wonder Leroy was getting so big; Ms Pompadore was feeding him entire loaves of bread.

As he passed over the wooden bridges and looked in at the orange-and-white fish swimming lazily in the ponds, Leo was certain that someone had been in the room before him, making all the trouble with the pipes.

But who?

It was seven thirty, and for the first time all day, everything in the Whippet Hotel was calm. It had taken Leo and his dad until then to do as Ms Sparks demanded upon her return from errands: "Put every guest request to rest!"

Not a bad turn of phrase for such a serious woman, and Leo had felt the distinct sense that Ms Sparks was in an unusually good mood. Maybe it was because dinner on the lawn had been cancelled due to lack of interest from the guests. This was a common occurrence given that there were six thousand restaurants one could visit in Manhattan and rich people were notorious foodies, always on the hunt for the next great restaurant. Food on the lawn at the Whippet was fine, but more than a few times a week was simply unimaginable, even for Captain Rickenbacker and Theodore Bump, who liked to order in from the finest establishments that would deliver.

And so it was that the Whippet was quiet as the hour of the dinner party arrived. Almost everyone, it seemed to Leo, was out at a restaurant of their own or holed up in their rooms playing pinball or writing romance novels.

"My dad is in the basement, but I've brought the purple box," Leo whispered into his radio. "Can you sneak away?"

Remi was still at the door and would be expected there all the way until eight, when Ms Sparks would finally relieve him of his duty.

"Ms Sparks is doing that head-bobbing thing, you know what I mean?"

"Seen it a thousand times," Leo answered. Usually around seven o'clock, Ms Sparks became sleepy. Her head would lean forwards until the giant beehive pointed at the door and then she'd pop back up again. The back and forth usually lasted about a half hour.

"Be right there," Remi said, and the radio went silent.

Leo was waiting on top of the duck elevator with the green and purple boxes. When he heard Remi enter the duck elevator below, there was only one question on Leo's mind.

"Did you get the blue box?"

"Leo?" Remi whispered. "Where are you?"

"Up here," said Leo, staring down through the trapdoor. "Shut the door and get up here – we've only got a few minutes before Ms Sparks goes looking for you."

Leo didn't see the blue box until Remi leaned out of the small space and pulled it in with him, handing it up through the hole.

"Nice work, Remi! You had me worried there for a second."

"Still no Blop, but at least we have the box back."

Remi closed the elevator and climbed up through the hole, sitting with his legs dangling back into the elevator.

"Better close the door up, just in case," said Leo.

The last thing they needed was Ms Sparks discovering the duck elevator had a secret door in its ceiling. The less she knew, the better.

Leo slid the blue box on top of the purple box, and Remi did the honours, pushing the green box into a set of slots atop the stack.

"They fit together just like we'd hoped," said Remi, sliding the elevator door shut and looking at the off-kilter collection of stacked boxes. "It's starting to look like the Whippet, don't you think?"

Leo had been thinking the same thing and nodded his agreement. The two boys stood up then, staring at the top of the green box.

"Here goes," said Leo, and he tried once more to slide the top off the box. This time it worked, and Leo pointed his maintenance torch inside.

"Whoa," Remi whispered, shadows and light filling the box. "It looks so real."

Leo didn't say anything at all, but he was just as mesmerized as Remi was. They'd opened a box to another world, and Leo could think of only one thing: *I hope we get to go there.*

Inside were three main things that caught the eye: a junkyard, a field of flowers and lots of flying objects. The junkyard was filled with tiny broken-down cars, refrigerators, motors and a thousand other objects in rolling piles. Leo leaned in very close, practically putting his head inside the green box, and saw tiny towers that reminded him of the teetering stacks of newspaper that stood next to his dad's bed, leaning as if they might fall at any moment. Remi reached in and touched one of the stacks of paper and found they weren't really paper at all, but small painted sculptures. Prehistoric metal creatures appeared to fly around the box, held up by wires, and the field of flowers covered half the floor with dazzling colours.

"This is a very strange box," said Remi. "What's it mean?"

Leo wasn't sure, so he pointed the torch to the underside of the lid, hoping for some clues. He was not disappointed.

"It's another note from Merganzer D Whippet," said Leo, and then he read it out loud.

A dark and dangerous path you seek.
Beware the holes, the bugs, the peak!
A flying goat will be of use.
Tipping cows, a ghost, apple juice.
Time is short, tonight's the night.

When all have gathered, make your flight!
    MDW
    PS. To get a Flying Farm key card, visit the
slug cave, turn the goat two times around, push.

Remi looked stricken. All this talk of haunted rooms and ghosts and dangerous paths was starting to make him nervous. "How well did you really know Mr Whippet?" he asked.

"Pretty well," said Leo. The two had been very close, which had made it all the more confusing and painful when Merganzer had suddenly disappeared without so much as a note.

"'A dark and dangerous path,'" said Remi. "Beware the holes and bugs? A ghost and a flying goat? You have to admit, it sounds like he's not the most normal duck in the pond."

"And you didn't mention the Flying Farm key card, which is super rare. Know what else?"

"What?"

"I've been in the slug cave. It's in the Haunted Room."

"Perfect."

Just then, the gate to the duck elevator swooshed open below them and Ms Sparks's voice boomed into the tiny space. "Remi! Door! Now!"

The two boys didn't move a muscle in their hiding spot on top of the duck elevator. What if Ms Sparks got hold of the boxes? What if she worked out what was going on? It would be the end of their adventure, the end of Remi working at the door, the end of Leo's dad working at the Whippet Hotel.

It would be the end of *everything*.

There was a stillness below, and Remi was sure he heard Ms Sparks sniffing the air.

"I smell pizza," she said. "Where are you?"

Ms Sparks crawled inside and started banging on the walls of the duck elevator. Her hair barely fitted inside and she had to turn very carefully from side to side as she pounded on the walls.

"I know you're in there! Remi!"

She was making a lot of noise, between the pounding and the yelling, but she went still as a statue when she hit the ceiling and felt the panel move ever so slightly.

"So that's your game," she whispered, grabbing the edge of the trapdoor and sliding it over violently. Her hairdo rose slowly up into the hole like a periscope. Her head followed, spinning round as she crawled like a dog on the floor of the duck elevator. Ms Sparks's eyes darted back and forth, her nose wrinkling at the smell of duck feathers and pizza.

But there was no one in the shaft to find.

Leo and Remi had fled into the maintenance tunnel with the boxes.

Milton knew how worried Bernard Frescobaldi could be when something big was about to happen. The hotel would soon change hands, and the pivotal moment had arrived.

"According to your schedule, we are to make our move tomorrow," said Milton. "Is that correct?"

Bernard was tired. It had been a demanding day, and he wasn't as young as he'd once been. So little time, so much left to do.

"If all goes as planned with you-know-who, tomorrow it is," said Bernard. "I have my doubts. You say they called again?"

"Oh yes, very enthusiastic," said Milton. "The ponds were a disaster and the paper clips worked exactly as we'd hoped. By all accounts, the Whippet is falling apart."

Milton saw that Bernard Frescobaldi was not comforted by this news, and added, "Which means the hotel could be fetched for a bargain price, as you'd planned."

"And yet it seems so peaceful over there," said Bernard. They'd parked across the street, staring at the iron gate.

"The boy and his father are efficient, I'll give them that," said Milton. "But they'll be extra distracted tonight. We'll hit them with a one-two punch that might just knock them out for good."

"We shall see," said Bernard. He glanced at Milton, who he thought was a bit too sure. "It's all set, then. Tomorrow we make our offer. Before someone else beats us to it."

The Whippet had the hotel equivalent of the flu, or so it seemed. Surely there were others watching, waiting for the perfect time to make a low offer, rip it down and build a skyscraper on the incredible site. It was, after all, Manhattan. That much property with such a tiny, exclusive hotel was an affront to every developer who drove by.

No, Bernard thought, it wouldn't be long. His plan was set in motion and the time had arrived. Come the next day, he'd make his offer and be done with it.

He pulled out the files on Merganzer D Whippet one last time and scanned the many papers, searching for a particularly troubling entry. He felt a twinge of regret, reading the private words of a man he sometimes understood, sometimes did not. A lunatic, a brilliant architect, a brokenhearted eccentric. Merganzer D Whippet was many things, but mostly, Bernard had come to believe, a good man with few regrets. A little sad, but mostly happy.

Milton looked at Bernard with mixed emotions. He'd known Bernard Frescobaldi a very long time. He'd been good to Milton, if challenging at times. If this is what he wanted, Milton would do everything he could to make sure it happened.

Milton watched as Bernard read the last letter once more, a letter that had been written one hundred and two days before, after which Merganzer D Whippet had disappeared from the hotel.

Merganzer D Whippet, the field

It took me a long time to understand what my father had meant. How wrong I'd been about those fateful words.

You will prosper in the field of wacky inventions.

I'd sold all of his buildings and all but one property, a forgotten country estate I'd never seen nor heard of. I'd spent many years building one hotel, with many invented things. And when my work was done, I sat on the roof with the ducks, looking at the city rising up all around me.

"I must go to see this last piece of property before I sell it."

And so I did.

I took my dear friend, George Powell, who by then was also managing most of my affairs. We drove out of the city and into the far upper reaches of New York State, armed only with a map and a duck. (Always bring a duck if you can. They are very useful creatures.)

We ventured out on to a distant country road dotted with cows and goats, until we came over a high bank and we both saw it off in the distance. We just . . . knew. It was my father's estate. It had to be. A high, rolling stone wall surrounding acres of land, and as we came near the gate, my heart sank.

The wall was old and falling down in places, overrun with weeds and thistles, crawling with green ivy. I had a key, which had been kept with the deed, and the key unlocked the high, arching metal door, rusted at the hinges.

We walked through the gate and my heart sank deeper still.

It had the appearance of a place that was to be, but never became, a place that had a special purpose, often thought of but never acted on.

There were no buildings, not one. Not a house or a red barn or a garage where a rich man might tinker with a foreign sports car he never intended to finish. But there were signs everywhere, expensive ones made of marble, like tombstones now, tipped over and dotting the acreage.

This is what the first one we came to said:

Here I will build a country house, where my wife and boy will play. And I will play with them, too. When my work is through.

Further still, another sign, the corner cracked and broken:

This is where the greenhouse will go, where my wife will grow rare orchids. And I will grow them, too. When my work is through.

And more:

The barn will go here, with horses my son will ride. And I will ride one, too. When my work is through.

The pond will go here, with ducks for Merganzer, because he loves ducks. And I love them, too. I'll love them best when my work is through.

And finally, we came to the saddest marble sign of all, the one that echoed my father's words down through the years. The largest plot remained.

And here I will make my field, a place with tools and sheds and tables of every kind, a field where we will imagine the wildest things in the summer sun, my boy and me. In the field of wacky inventions, my boy will prosper. And I will, too. When my work is through.

I stood in that open field, watching the wind blow through the tall weeds, and my good friend, George, put an arm around me. We cried for what never was and what could never be.

"His heart was in the right place after all," George said.

It was just the sort of thing a best friend should say.

I believe he was right.

MDW

· CHAPTER 11 ·

A HAUNTED DINNER PARTY

Leo showed Remi how to double back through the maintenance tunnel into the grounds through a trapdoor in the gardening shed. Unfortunately for Remi, when he opened the trapdoor, Mr Phipps was in the shed, sharpening his shears.

"Lost?" asked the old gardener, sliding a blade across a big stone on a bench without even a glance at Remi.

Remi thought he might run, but what he really needed was an alibi.

"I was helping Leo. He showed me the way out."

"Uh-huh," said Mr Phipps, holding the shears in

the light and running his finger along an edge. Remi gulped.

"Anyway, you know how Ms Sparks can be. She hates Leo. Any chance I could say you needed some help out here instead?"

Mr Phipps looked at Remi then, one dark eyebrow raised, and Remi crumbled.

"It's only my second day on the job, Mr Phipps. My mum will kill me if I get fired."

Mr Phipps smiled, laughed soft and deep, and waved his hand towards the door.

"Better get back where you belong – tell Ms Sparks I needed help moving dirt bags."

"Wow, thanks, Mr Phipps! I totally owe you one."

Remi dug into his pocket and held out the smashed remains of his pizza, which Mr Phipps gladly accepted. Remi ran with all his might, the red jacket flapping up behind him in the wind. He waited outside the hotel door to catch his breath, then went inside and found that Ms Sparks had returned.

"Mr Phipps needed help," Remi blurted. He was a lousy liar. "You were sleeping so I didn't want to wake you."

Ms Sparks was fuming mad, but what could she say? She'd been caught snoozing.

"You and that maintenance boy are up to no good. Don't think I don't know."

"His name is Leo," said Remi.

Ms Sparks stared down at Remi with a look that said *Of course I know his name is Leo! I just don't care!*

Ten minutes later, she let Remi off for the night with a stern warning about sneaking around, and soon after that he was standing on the eighth-floor landing with Leo, late by fifteen minutes for the dinner party they'd been invited to.

"Are you ready?" asked Leo, who had put on his one and only suit and tie, a sad little affair that made Remi laugh.

"Trust me, yours isn't much better," said Leo, pointing out that Remi was wearing a red-and-white monkey suit.

"You got me there," said Remi, and then added, "Do you think he'll be in there?"

"You mean Merganzer?"

"Yeah, the main mystery dude."

Leo shrugged his shoulders, hoping that would be exactly who they would see inside. He had already imagined the dinner party. It would be Merganzer D Whippet, Leo, Remi and Betty. The four of them would talk about *everything* (Betty would quack a lot): all the hidden floors, all the mysteries of the hotel.

"Here we go," said Leo, taking the skull-and-cross-bones knocker in his hand and whacking it against the door three times.

The door began to open, and Remi saw the darkness and shadows inside. He started back-pedalling towards the stairs and bumped into something, which made him scream. LillyAnn Pompadore had come up the stairs, half out of breath. She was holding Hiney in one arm as she touched up her hair with the other.

"Oh, good," she said, brushing past Remi as if he didn't exist. "I hate to be the last one at a party, and I'm running terribly late."

Before Leo and Remi could say a word, Ms Pompadore had gone through the door and slammed it shut.

"What's *she* doing in there?" asked Leo. "You don't think she was actually *invited*?"

Remi shrugged, stepping forwards and knocking on the door once more.

"Hey, if she can do it, I can definitely do it. Let's go in and see what this is all about."

Leo's heart was broken. He'd made the mistake of letting himself get excited about seeing Merganzer again, but it was beginning to look as if the invite list for the party was anything but exclusive.

The door opened, and this time the two boys went inside the Haunted Room. It was the least-rented floor in the entire hotel; in fact, the rumour was that it had never been rented. Not even once. When the door slammed behind them, Remi could see why.

"It's dark in here," he whispered. "And spooky."

A collection of bats – were they real or mechanical? – flew low overhead, screeching as the boys ran further into the gloom. A dark blue moon hovered in a cloudy sky as the shadow of a werewolf crept into the moss-encrusted trees. The shadow (or whatever was *making* the shadow) growled, baring its huge, shadowy teeth.

"I can see why this room isn't very popular," said Remi, practically jumping into Leo's arms.

"Just remember it's all fake and you'll be fine," said Leo. "It's like a haunted house. Embrace it."

"It's all fake, nothing is real," Remi repeated over and over.

They heard voices, which they followed, and

entered a dreary clearing with a long stone table.

"This can't be," whispered Leo, for the table was very full of people. All the long-term guests were there, even Theodore Bump and the Yanceys.

"*Mum?*" said Remi.

"Remilio!" She beamed with pleasure at the sight of her son. She stood up nervously, still in her maid's uniform.

Clarence Fillmore was also there, sitting across from Remi's mum.

"What's going on here?" The question came from Leo and Remi at the same time.

"All the invitations were the same," said Mr Fillmore, holding up an envelope. It wasn't tiny, like the one Leo and Remi had got. It was a normal size. A lot of the other guests held up their invitations, too, and Leo's dad read his.

"'Party on the eighth floor, tell no one! Arrive 8 p.m. sharp.'"

"Really, I was only going to stop in for a moment," Pilar said again, feeling awful for not telling her own son. "Mostly out of curiosity."

Clarence Fillmore nodded the same, but little Jane Yancey felt differently. "I don't know why the servants get to come, especially *those* two." She pointed in Leo and Remi's general direction. "It's a hotel, Daddy. It's for *guests*."

The chandelier over the table fell half a metre and jerked to a stop, sending all the guests into a fit of screaming and laughter.

Jane Yancey glared at Leo. "Hey, Mr Maintenance Man, your light fell down. Aren't you going to fix it?"

There was one thing Leo and Remi were starting to realize about Jane Yancey: it took a lot to scare her.

A single bat flew over the table and disappeared in a burst of flame. When the smoke cleared, Count Dracula was standing at the head of the table. Jane Yancey rolled her eyes as Dracula spoke.

"Dinner is served."

The restaurant staff was dressed in black – grim butlers and maids – and they began serving the first course.

Remi and Leo couldn't help notice their parents were sitting across from each other, ignoring everyone else at the table.

"I think I'll show Remi around the Haunted Room," said Leo. "We're not hungry."

"But . . ." said Remi, thinking of how little he'd eaten all day. He looked at Leo and could tell he didn't want to sit at the long stone table and talk to a bunch of grown-ups. Besides, they were there for a reason the others weren't: they had to find a Flying Farm key card.

The two headed down a dark path sparkling with fireflies, and when they were out of earshot, Leo reminded Remi of Merganzer's words.

"Don't you remember, from the box?" he whispered. "'When all are gathered, make your flight.' This whole thing is a setup so we can move around the hotel unseen."

"He's helping us!" Remi said too loudly, which was followed by the sound of a witch cackling, off in the woods.

"Not everyone's here," said Leo, who was less enthusiastic than Remi. "I didn't see Ms Sparks or Mr Phipps."

Remi punched Leo in a friendly sort of way. "Even Merganzer wouldn't invite that old witch to a party, and Mr Phipps goes to bed at, like, seven thirty. Dude's probably sleeping."

"Either way, we need to get out of here," said Leo. "It's what the box said."

"Right, *focus*," said Remi. "We got this."

Just as he said *We got this*, a gathering of zombies started following them on the path. Two more appeared in front of them.

"We're trapped!" yelled Remi.

"Remi, please, try to remember. It's all *fake*."

Leo walked up to one of the approaching zombies and brushed it aside. Its arm fell off and Remi shuddered, but Leo picked it up and tossed it into the gloomy trees. All the zombies followed after it.

"This is the weirdest hotel room *ever*," said Remi.

"That's what you said about the last one."

"Yeah, but this time I really mean it."

They arrived at the opening of a narrow tunnel, which would require getting down on their knees. A creepy slurping sound came from inside.

"No way," said Remi. "Not gonna happen. Whatever's in there will eat my face off."

"For crying out loud, Remi," said Leo, sitting down in front of the opening and patting the ground. "Come on, sit down. Let's just take a break and get you back in the game."

Remi sat on the far side of Leo, away from the opening, and a spider the size of a tennis ball drifted down in front of his face. Remi was having some trouble breathing until Leo batted it away with his hand and it went scurrying into the dark.

"You're a braver man than I am," said Remi. "I don't know how you do it."

"I've been in here with Merganzer about a hundred times," Leo offered. "I'm telling you, it's all mechanical."

He glanced at Remi and felt sorry for him.

"The first time I came in here, I came close to peeing my pants."

"You're just trying to make me feel better," said Remi.

"No, honestly. It was pathetic."

Remi started laughing as the mechanical spider crawled up next to his leg.

"Hey, little fella," he said, picking it up by its back as the legs searched for a footing. Once he had hold of it, the spider wasn't so bad. The fact that it was robotic turned it from scary to cool in a hurry.

"Where's your favourite place to go, besides the Whippet Hotel?" asked Remi, touching the legs and finding they were cold.

"The New York Public Library," Leo said without the slightest hesitation. It came to him instantly, but saying it sort of made him sad.

"You like books, huh?"

Leo sighed deeply, listening to the fake wind rustle through the fake trees.

"Yeah, I like books. We didn't – well, we *don't*

have much money. My mum used to take me to the library every Saturday. I think I liked the books more than she did."

Remi knew Leo's mum had passed away a few years back; his own mother had told him that much. *Touchy subject*, she'd said. *Tread lightly*.

"Your dad doesn't take you? I mean, you know, since . . ."

Remi felt like he'd totally blown it, but Leo didn't mind.

"He has a hard time going to places we used to go. But I think he might finally be feeling a little better." Leo looked off towards the table, imagining his dad talking to Pilar. He thought of the ring he'd got back for him. Maybe his dad was almost ready to start living again.

"You're lucky," said Remi, setting down the giant spider, which clung to his leg. "You get to live in this place all the time."

Remi was nervous about saying anything more, because he'd always worried his friends would judge him if he told the truth.

"It's a pretty good gig, I have to admit," said Leo. "Where do you live? What's your dad do?"

Remi didn't say anything for a few seconds, and

Leo thought maybe he should just crawl into the cave and forget about it.

"Staten Island. That's where we live," Remi blurted out. "After work we take the subway to Battery Park, then catch the ferry, then hoof it to a crummy old building, then hoof it up the stairs to a crummy little apartment. Dad's not in the picture."

There, he'd said it.

"Must take a while to get home," said Leo, adding it up in his head.

"An hour and a half here, an hour and a half back, but it's a good job and Mum needs it."

Leo was about to say he would talk to his dad and see if maybe something could be worked out, but before he could say anything, he saw Jane Yancey walking towards them on the path.

"I give her points for being brave," whispered Leo. "Nothing scares that kid."

"Wanna bet?" asked Remi, picking up the spider.

"You wouldn't."

Jane Yancey marched right up and stood in front of them with her hands on her hips.

"I bet you're both too chicken to go in there," she said, staring at the hole and hearing the noise.

"You got that right," said Remi. "No way *we're* going in there."

Jane looked at Remi like he was the most pathetic kid on planet Earth and crouched in front of the hole. As soon as she started crawling inside, Remi set the giant spider on her back.

Jane backed out of the hole and stood up. She had a strange look on her face. The spider crawled up on top of her head, then down on to her face.

Then Jane Yancey screamed and ran away.

"I guess there *is* something that scares that kid," said Leo.

"Come on! Let's get out of here while the going is good."

Remi went first, then Leo, and before they knew it, they'd passed the thirty-centimetre-long slurping cave slugs and entered a small room with a glowing floor.

"There," said Leo. "On the wall."

"You're sure this is going to work?"

"I'm never sure of anything in the Whippet, but the box made it clear: *slug cave, turn the goat two times around, push*."

There were hieroglyphics of flying animals on the walls, one of which was a goat with wings far too small to lift it off the ground. Leo covered the goat with his palm, turned his hand twice and pushed. The flying goat spun once, then twice, followed by a *baaaah* sound from the ceiling.

"Is that it?" asked Remi, staring up into the high arch of the cave. "The Flying Farm key card?"

Leo nodded. "Very rare. And very high."

The key had descended out of a crack in the stone and fallen free, only to be caught on a bed of cobwebs high overhead. The key card had a dairy cow pattern on it, white with black splotches.

Remi piped in, "Let me guess – fake cobwebs from the fake spider crawling on Jane Yancey's face."

"You guessed it."

Remi jumped but came up short by at least half a metre.

"Get on my back," he said. "You can reach it from up there."

Remi leaned over and Leo climbed aboard, standing on Remi's shoulders. He still couldn't reach it, so he leapt into the air, knocking Remi into a ninja death roll. After they both tumbled on to the floor of the cave, they sat up, only to find Jane Yancey standing at the exit, her arms crossed over her six-year-old chest.

"You put that spider on my back. I *know* you did! I hope you had a good laugh because I'm telling my father, and when I do, *both* your parents are going to lose their jobs. What do you think of that, Spider Boy and Dumb Face?"

It was all Leo could do not to tie up Jane Yancey and leave her with the slugs, but he stayed calm, looked at Remi, and shrugged.

"Which one of us is Spider Boy?" asked Remi.

"Forget Spider Boy! You're BOTH Dumb Faces!"

Remi knelt down next to Jane Yancey and looked her in the eye. "I think someone of your ability could be useful to us. Have you ever done any spying?"

Leo couldn't believe his ears. "You really are a Dumb Face."

Jane, intrigued by Remi's question, looked at Leo. "Your *dad* is a Dumb Face."

Leo realized the entire situation was becoming ridiculous. He would not stoop to Jane Yancey's level. Instead of Dumb-Facing her back, he said, "We're pretty sure Ms Sparks is a double-agent superspy who wants to take over the hotel, hit it with a wrecking ball and build a fur coat factory in its place."

This was, in a word, brilliant. There wasn't a six-year-old in Manhattan who didn't hate the idea of fur coats, given that they always came from cuddly animals.

Jane Yancey looked them both over carefully, searching for signs of deceit. Finding none, she put out her hand.

"Partners."

Remi shook Jane Yancey's sticky little hand, then gave her a mission.

"Keep an eye on Ms Sparks," he said. "If she tries to follow us, you'll know we're in trouble, since we're the good guys."

"*Obviously*," said Leo. "We're the good guys."

Jane scowled at Leo, then returned her gaze to Remi. "I'm good at following people around and shin-kicking."

"I bet you are," said Leo.

Jane Yancey hauled off and kicked Leo in the shin, which felt about the same as being whacked with a baseball bat.

"See, told you so."

She laughed at Leo as he jumped around the cave, then she crawled away in search of Ms Sparks.

Remi laughed at Leo, but only a little.

"She'll follow you around all the time," said Leo,

rubbing the sting out of his shin. "Getting kicked was a better deal."

Remi agreed Leo was probably right, then looked up at the ceiling, expecting to see the Flying Farm key card.

"Already got it," said Leo, holding the cow-patterned card out for Remi to see. "Let's get out of here before she comes back with a weapon. I have a feeling we've created a monster."

· CHAPTER 12 ·

THE FLYING FARM ROOM

Leo had a feeling about needing a duck. He couldn't say why, other than the fact that Merganzer had always believed that a journey with a duck was safer than a journey without one. But it was more than that. They were exploring the higher levels of the Whippet Hotel, which had always seemed more unpredictable than the lower levels. And Leo had a bad feeling about the Flying Farm Room, a notoriously confusing place. He needed all the backup he could get.

And so, after sneaking away from the haunted dinner party, Leo had taken Remi through the maintenance tunnels, into the duck elevator, and up to the roof, detouring their entire plan by a half hour in order to retrieve Betty. She was not happy to be bothered, and Leo thought, once again, how crabby this particular duck had become of late.

Without Merganzer's silver key card, the Flying Farm Room was only accessible by using Flying Farm key cards. The key cards weren't made in the usual way, so they were tough to come by. Ms Sparks kept them in a safe in her room, and they were only handed out on exceptional occasions. In the past, when someone stayed in the room (extraordinarily rarely), Merganzer D Whippet had attended to the room himself, making sure every detail was in order. Certainly no one had stayed in the room since Mr Whippet's disappearance, and this worried Leo greatly.

"I've only been in this room once before," he said, standing in front of the door with his friend and his duck. "It was a tad . . . wild. I can only imagine what it must be like now. I don't think anyone has been in here in quite a while."

"It can't be any worse than the Haunted Room," Remi said. "That place gave me the creeps."

Leo stood back a moment and looked all around, thinking how far they'd come. They were on the ninth floor. Beyond that lay the roof, and between the ninth floor and the roof there was the possibility of a tenth floor that no one but Merganzer had ever seen, not even the maintenance men.

"We've worked our way to the top of the Whippet," Leo observed.

"I was just thinking the same thing," said Remi. "Nine floors. Plus the hidden floors – how many are there?"

Leo counted in his head: the Room of Rings or the Ring of Rooms, the Railway Room and the secret room they hadn't found yet. "I count thirteen, if you include the basement."

"Not the luckiest number," Remi said. "Maybe there's another hidden floor."

"Or a hundred more."

Leo had been making a joke, but saying it made it seem possible. Maybe there were more rooms than either one of them could imagine.

Betty quacked, nipping at Leo's trouser leg.

"Something's wrong with your duck," Remi noticed. "Are you sure we should take her with us?"

"I'm sure," said Leo. "Let's get going before someone finds us."

He placed the Flying Farm key card in the slot.

The key disappeared, the door made a *baaaah* noise, and a new key card appeared. It was grey, with a goat face and words printed on it:

Come right in, we've been waiting for you.

Leo thought the note had an ominous feel to it.

"This is weird," said Remi, but he went right in, just like the card said he should. Leo took the grey key card and put it in the pocket of his dinner jacket, which he had failed to shed after the dinner party. He wished he'd had time to stop in the basement and put his overalls back on. The suit was itchy and uncomfortable, plus it lacked the many tools he preferred to carry around with him. Tools, he had found, were a comfort on an unpredictable journey.

The door unlocked and they slipped through, captivated by what lay on the other side. They would have been smart to pay closer attention as the door swung slowly shut, because it didn't quite shut all the way. Someone was in the hall, the toe of a boot holding the door open by the tiniest of cracks.

As Leo and Remi entered the Flying Farm Room, Remi dived for the floor, which was bright green and soft like grass.

"Whoa! Heads up!" he yelled, but since Leo had been in the room once before, he knew a few things Remi did not. Betty waddled out into the Flying Farm without them, apparently in search of a pond or a loaf of pumpernickel.

"Was that a flying pig or have I lost my mind?" asked Remi.

"Just remember, none of this is real."

"It looked plenty real to me. That pig just about knocked me off my feet."

Remi stood up again and the two boys looked across the long room. The ceiling was only three metres overhead, but it looked for all the world like an endless blue sky dotted with white clouds.

Then Remi was back on the turf, dodging a herd of oncoming sheep that had cannonballed from the sky. There were eleven of them in a V formation, and they were faster than the pig had been. Remi was pretty sure he heard them laughing as they whooshed past like eleven wool-covered fighter planes.

"These flying farm animals play rough!" Remi yelled, but Leo was still standing, looking towards a fenced-in area way off in the corner of the room. He didn't seem to take much notice of the flying pigs, sheep, or even the flying bull that was heading right towards them, spewing fire from its nose.

"Um, Leo? Please tell me you know something I don't. Otherwise a two-thousand-pound fire-breathing bull is about to ram us into the turf!"

Remi cowered as the bull landed three feet away, preparing to charge right over the top of them both.

"It's been nice knowing you, Leo. Tell my mum I love her, and kick Jane Yancey in the shin for me."

Leo was tempted to let the ruse go a little longer, but they had work to do. Playing with the animals would have to wait.

"Everything up there – the sky, the flying animals – it's all fake, remember?" said Leo.

"Even if it's a fancy robot, it's still a fancy robot BULL!" said Remi, opening his eyes and turning back to the huge beast, which was now centimetres from his face.

"You can pet it if you want," said Leo. "It won't hurt you."

But the bull looked so real – everything did – that Remi just couldn't bring himself to do anything but stay curled up in a ball.

"Oh, for crying out loud," said Leo, stepping towards the bull and reaching his hand out to its fire-breathing face.

"No! Don't do it, Leo! It'll fry your arm off!"

"Just watch," said Leo, and Remi peeked through his fingers, which were covering his face. When Leo reached out, his hand went right through the bull's head. He walked around the beast, sweeping his hand through its monstrous body, then slapped it on the behind. The bull reared up on two legs, slamming down on top of Remi.

"It's a hologram," said Leo. "Everything in the sky – *including* the sky – they're all holograms."

Remi reached out his hand and ran it through the flames shooting out of the bull's nose.

"I am the happiest kid in New York City," said Remi, swishing his hands back and forth through the bull's legs. He got up and started taunting the bull, just for fun.

"We don't really have time to play with the animals right now," said Leo. "We have to find that hidden room. And I think I know how."

Leo and Remi walked through the middle of the Flying Farm with its rolling hills of Astroturf, its split-rail fences, and the sounds of animals all around them. Betty was honking at a herd of six goats that was flying around a red barn (which was also the master bedroom) and Leo called for her to follow.

He'd been thinking about the fence around the cows, and how the cows weren't moving.

"Let me have a look at that new key card," Remi said, seeing the herd of goats land on the red barn and begin eating the shingles off the roof. Leo gave him the card, warning Remi to be very quiet if he could. They were approaching a group of sleeping cows, their wings fluttering softly.

"But cows don't sleep during the day," said Remi.

He'd never been to a real farm in his life, but even he knew cows only slept at night, and were easily startled.

Leo shrugged. "I guess flying cows sleep during the day and fly around at night. How am I supposed to know?"

Remi examined the goat key card more carefully, and noticed that there was a button on the edge, similar to one on a cell phone. He pushed the button and the key card came to life as a touch screen.

"Leo, you gotta see this," said Remi. Leo and Remi huddled over the screen, which showed the floor plan of the room. It also showed one goat, sitting on the roof of the red barn.

"Do you suppose . . . ?" asked Remi, putting his finger on the screen and sliding the goat away from the barn and out over the green grass. The two boys looked back at the real barn and saw that one goat had flown away, following wherever Remi moved his finger along the screen.

"This must be the goat we're looking for," said Leo, thinking of the words from the lid of the last box:

A flying goat will be of use.

"His name is Merle," said Remi, bringing the goat up close and seeing he had a name-tag around his neck.

"Welcome to the adventure, Merle," Leo whispered. "Be as quiet as a mouse."

Merle *baaaah*ed softly.

"Shhhhhhhh," said Leo as they approached the pasture gate. "We'll need to tip them over."

Remi knew that it was wrong to tip cows over in real life – they had a hard time getting back up, making it a pretty cruel thing to do. But *virtual* cow-tipping sounded like a lot of fun to Remi, and he hoped that a holographic cow would tip as well as a real one. They left Betty and Merle behind, hoping they wouldn't quack and *baaaah* too much, and tiptoed into the pasture. The cows all had their heads down, eyes closed, giant chests heaving slowly.

"Ready?" Leo whispered.

Remi put the goat key card in his red jacket pocket and nodded.

Leo signalled with his fingers. *One . . . two . . . three!*

They pushed the biggest cow, and though their hands went right through, the cow still fell over on its side with a loud *thud*. As soon as it did, its wings began flapping wildly, waking up the other five cows. Confused, they flew into one another, bouncing back and forth until the one the boys had tipped over bounced into the ceiling and a familiar sight appeared.

"I never thought I'd see a hole in the sky," said Remi, and that's exactly what it looked like. A ladder shot down, touching the Astroturf in the pasture, and the hole in the sky waited.

The cows flew off noisily in the direction of the front door as Leo ran back to the gate.

"I'll get Betty. You get Merle up the hole as fast as you can."

Remi had Merle up and out of sight in no time at all, but Leo had trouble with Betty. It wasn't like her to run away from him, but he found himself chasing

Betty around the red barn, when he heard a terrible sound.

Someone was putting a key card into the door.

"Remi! Get down!" yelled Leo, catching Betty and swerving into the barn for cover. When Leo peeked around the corner, he saw a tall beehive hairdo leaning into the room.

Ms Sparks had found them.

"I know you're in here," she taunted. "I can smell pizza."

Remi, who was hiding in the cow pasture, sniffed the air around him, and wondered if it was true. Even though he'd given it to Mr Phipps, he'd carried his lunch around in his pocket for a long time.

Leo was holding Betty's bill shut, but she was a strong duck and she kept swinging her powerful neck back and forth.

"I'm going to count to three," said Ms Sparks, batting away an annoying pig that was trying to land in her hair. She, like Leo, knew the animals in the Flying Farm weren't real. "I despise the Flying Farm," she said under her breath, and then started to count.

"ONE!" She took several steps into the room.

"TWO!" She took a few more steps, nearing the red barn.

She was about to say THREE! when Betty finally got her bill free from Leo's hand and honked, loudly, right in his face.

"Run for it!" yelled Leo, and Remi was up in a flash, heading for the ladder.

"HOLD IT RIGHT THERE!" screamed Ms Sparks, stepping on a holographic cow pie the size of a Frisbee.

Leo ran out of the barn, carrying Betty like a football. Ms Sparks was about to give chase, but she didn't have a chance.

Jane Yancey darted out in front of her, one hand on her hip and one behind her back.

"I caught you!" the rich little girl proclaimed. Ms Sparks wasn't sure what to do. The girl's father was a zillionaire.

"You keep all these exotic animals up here so you can get their fur!" yelled Jane Yancey. She kicked Ms Sparks in the shin, then pulled the giant spider out from behind her back and threw it into the beehive hairdo. Ms Sparks, unaware of the earlier dinner party and mortally afraid of spiders, flung her head violently back and forth. The herd of flying sheep circled the beehive. The bull charged.

It was mayhem in the Flying Farm Room.

"That'll teach you!" said Jane Yancey. "I'm telling my dad you're running a secret fur farm in this hotel!" She marched right out of the room and slammed the door.

Ms Sparks ran behind her, a menagerie of flying animals tailing her and a giant mechanical spider latched on to her beehive.

When she looked back one last time, Leo and Remi were gone.

It was as if they'd never been there to begin with.

· CHAPTER 13 ·

THE GHOST ORCHID

"I know what this is."

Betty quacked at the sound of Leo's voice, but she had grown timid after being put down. Something about the room didn't agree with her.

"How could anyone know what *this* is?" asked Remi. Merle the flying goat hovered over Betty's head, watching the duck curiously.

"My grandpa, the one on my mum's side, he was a rat," said Leo.

"And you're telling me this because . . . ?"

Leo stepped out into the maze. "His apartment was so full of junk, it made a path that wound from room to room. Do you know what they call a thing like that?"

"A junkyard?"

"No, Remi, not a junkyard. It's called a goat trail, and that's exactly what this is."

The two boys gazed into the maze, which was oddly frightening to behold. The entire thing appeared to be made of junk, pile after pile, rising all the way to the ceiling. Chairs, old dishwashers, cans of paint, picture frames, books, shelves, computers, telephones, car tyres – it went on and on and on, and it all looked as if it might crumble to the floor at any moment.

"Do you hear that?" Remi asked.

The junk was moving, like the sound of a very old boat on a windswept pond.

"I have a feeling we'd better not touch any of it," said Leo.

The goat trail was narrow, barely wide enough for two boys, a duck and a flying goat to pass in single file.

"Hey, Leo, check this out."

Remi held the grey key card out so Leo could see it. The touch screen had changed.

"Now I see why we needed a flying goat," said Leo. Betty quacked as if to say *Merle's not the only one that can fly around here, you know!*

"There's the end," said Remi, touching a flashing green arrow at the far end of the screen. He might have been more intelligent to point, not touch, because Merle was gone around the first corner of the goat trail before they could stop him.

Remi was just about to push on the start of the maze again and call Merle back when Leo grabbed him by the arm and pulled him into the maze.

"RUN!"

The towering junk teetered back and forth and started to crumble, then the entryway to the maze came crashing down as Betty took flight and landed in Leo's arms. An old bicycle seat flew through the air and hit Leo in the back of the head. It was a soft seat, but it hit him hard, knocking him forwards as Betty sprang free and flew away.

"Leo! Don't move!" yelled Remi. They'd come round the first corner, and the junk was no longer only on both sides of them. Remi was the first to see that the junk was now over the top of them as well. They were trapped in a cocoon of garage-sale cast-offs. One false move and the whole room would come crashing down on top of them both.

"I'm okay, in case you were interested," said Leo, rubbing the back of his head as he sat up.

"Glad to hear it."

Both boys sat on the floor, staring at the fallen entryway, as Remi called Merle back with a touch of his finger. The key card screen now showed their progress, so he knew where to touch, and Merle was hovering overhead a few seconds later.

"There's only one pathway out of this crazy thing," said Leo, staring down the narrow goat trail that branched out like veins in every direction. "Good thing we have a flying goat that can lead the way."

"You said it, brother," Remi offered. He hadn't meant it to sound like they really were brothers, but they both smiled awkwardly at the idea, anyway.

"Where's Betty?" asked Leo, suddenly realizing the duck was gone.

They both worried over which path she might have flown down, and Leo felt especially terrible.

"I never should have brought her in here. If she gets turned around, she'll never find her way out."

Remi sent Merle back towards the exit and they followed, careful not to touch the walls as they went. Each time Merle got too far ahead of them, Remi called him back with a touch of his finger. They went on like this – in circles, it seemed – for some time, until Leo heard a loud crash somewhere off to his left. Both boys could only think of one thing, but neither of them would say it. *Betty*.

"Let's just keep moving – we'll find her," said Remi. And so they did.

Ten minutes later, Leo was sure they'd come back to the same spot.

"I saw that mailbox a while back," he said, pointing to a rusted-out box without a door, holding someone's old mail.

They heard another crash, this time on the right, and the floor started to move.

"This can't be good," said Remi, balancing as his feet wobbled back and forth. He put the grey key card in his pocket for safe keeping just as the floor gave way in a perfect circle three metres back. The circle was about sixty centimetres across, the path they stood on falling away into black. A second later, another hole caved in. Then another.

"Those holes are chasing us!" yelled Leo. "Which way?"

They'd come to a fork in the path. Remi pulled the key card out of his pocket once more, but Merle was at the exit again. The card had told Merle where to go, but the flying goat was so far ahead, he'd left Leo and Remi wondering where to turn.

"I can't remember which way to go!" Remi said, three more holes appearing behind them.

Leo looked in both directions. If he chose wrong, the holes might chase them into a dead end and swallow them up.

"I say left," said Remi.

"I was thinking the same thing," said Leo.

"At least we'll be right or wrong together!"

As a hole dropped through right behind them, Leo lost his footing and began falling back. Remi grabbed Leo by the hand and pulled as he felt the floor shifting under his feet. Two seconds, maybe three, and a hole would appear, dragging them both under. Remi pulled as hard as he could and dived down the path.

Leo landed on top of Remi, then accidentally batted the wall of junk with his hand. The ceiling made a horrible grinding noise as everything shifted. Both boys closed their eyes tight, waiting for the end.

Three seconds passed, then five, then ten. The ceiling, it appeared, was going to hold.

"You dived *right*," said Leo, sitting up and seeing where they'd landed, right on the edge of the Y in the path. The holes had continued to the left as far as he could see.

"Good thing you almost fell into that hole or we'd both be goners."

Leo and Remi stood up, called Merle back and worried about Betty.

"You probably saved my life right there," said Leo as they kept walking. "How about I take you to the Cake Room when we get out of here?"

"Now you're talking!"

Merle returned very quickly this time, which told them something important: they were near the end of the goat trail. In fact, as they came around the next corner, they could see the exit, which bothered them both.

"We can't leave Betty in here," said Leo. "What would Merganzer think?"

But they needn't have worried so much. They heard Betty's familiar quack, and it wasn't coming from anywhere behind them. It was coming from somewhere beyond the exit.

"Smart duck you got there," said Remi.

"No doubt," Leo answered, and they both followed Merle to the end of the path. The closer they got, the more they both thought they heard a new sound, like rusty scissors opening and closing. It did not strike either of them as a good sound.

"Do you see that?" asked Remi, stopping in his tracks.

"I do," said Leo, and then they both started running.

The old sinks and pots and dressers were moving, not towards them, but *away* from them.

The wall of junk was coming alive.

"Bad flying creatures!" yelled Remi. "Bad bad bad!"

They'd run with everything they had to the exit, watching as toasters and tricycles and everything else sprang to life and began flying overhead. Like a host of sleeping prehistoric flying beasts, the walls and the ceiling woke up, screeching their terrible wings over a field of flowers. Behind them, the entire maze fell to the floor with a great crash, and Leo had to wonder whether or not the whole hotel wouldn't fall down with it. Behind them lay a junkyard, before them a pristine field of flowers, over their heads an unimaginable sky of flying garbage.

"Are they mechanical or are they holograms?" Remi asked, hoping against all hope for the latter.

"I've never been in here before. I have no idea!" Leo answered. But then a flying picture frame slammed into the junk pile, sparks of glass flying every where.

"I think that answers our question," said Remi. "This stuff is real! We're dead!"

They stood at the edge of the junkyard as crazy flying creatures guarded the field of flowers. Merle had joined in and the key card had gone totally blank, so they weren't getting any more help from the flying goat.

"What are we supposed to do?" asked Remi. The key card began to vibrate in his hand, and the black screen wasn't totally black any more. It looked as though someone was inside the card, writing on the screen with his finger, as if the screen were filled with black soot and it could be wiped away from another world that lay hidden in the card.

"Um, Leo, you better check this out."

Leo ducked as a giant bug with a popcorn popper for a head did a kamikaze dive, crashing into the debris with a flash of sparks. He leaned in close to the screen and watched as a message appeared.

Always good to have a duck.
DUCK!

Both boys looked up and saw a swarm of flying metal insects, all of them made of bits of scissors, diving towards them. They ducked to the floor in the nick of time and the bugs exploded against the junk pile, raining down scissors as Leo and Remi rolled out of the way.

"We were almost kebabs!" yelled Remi. "I don't know about you, but I don't want to be the main course at the next Whippet Hotel barbecue."

"I'm with you," said Leo, and he whistled three times fast, the same whistle his father had used in the hotel lobby when Betty and her buddies had gone berserk. The sound echoed through the room, and off in the distance, at the far end of the field of flowers, a tiny duck head popped up.

Betty quacked.

Then she ran and took flight, calling out wildly as she careered around the room. The flying junk gathered in a line behind her, as if it were being called to follow and Betty was its leader. She flew around and around until all the rubbish followed her like a long, whipping tail.

"Go, Betty, go!" Remi yelled. And go she did, over the junkyard, swooping high, then diving straight down. She turned at the last second, and every flying creature slammed one by one into the scrap pile.

All was quiet then, but for the sound of Betty's

wings as she flew overhead and back to where she'd come from at the other end of the room. A moment later, she landed in the tall flowers and Leo couldn't see her any more.

"I have a feeling she knows where we're supposed to go," he said.

Remi just shook his head. "'Always bring a duck.' Words to live by."

The room felt deathly still as they walked a thin path through a field of orchids.

"These are hard to grow," said Leo, having a sudden memory he'd all but forgotten.

"How do you know that?"

"They're orchids. They need special care." The memory flooded back now as Leo reached out and touched the weirdly shaped flowers. Some were orange, some red, some blue, and all of them had long green stems and oddly shaped petals.

"My mum tried to grow them once in our living room, under a lamp," said Leo, a dreaminess to his voice that Remi hadn't heard before. "She said it would make our flat feel like magic. And it did. I remember now, she *did* grow an orchid."

"Only one?" asked Remi. But looking at the flowers, he could see how just one would be enough to make his own crummy flat feel magical.

"Remi, I know what the ghost is," said Leo, a tingle in his voice.

"What ghost?"

"The one from the box, remember? 'Tipping cows, a ghost, apple juice.'"

"Yeah, that one's had me stumped."

Leo didn't answer; he simply kept on down the path, looking back and forth over the field of orchids. As they approached the end of the path, the garden turned swampy and they waded through thirty centimetres of water with fallen trees strewn about.

"Do you smell that?" asked Remi. "Smells like apple juice."

"That means it's blooming," said Leo, spotting Betty lolling in the water contentedly. She was swimming around under a branch, and on the branch sat a perfectly white box with its lid open.

Light was coming out of the box.

"Hold on a second, Leo. The finger is back."

Remi held out the key card so Leo could see, as it vibrated, the screen filling once more with black.

"By the way, whoever's in the card, they can see us," said Remi. He'd been thinking about it a lot. "How else would they have known to say 'DUCK'?"

Leo looked all around, expecting to see Mr M hiding somewhere, but he did not.

The finger drew a message, then crossed part of it out.

The box is for ~~Leo~~.

"Looks like I might get this one," said Remi. "I wonder why?"

But that was not to be. Instead, the finger filled in a different name.

The box is for ~~Leo~~ Clarence.

Remi looked at Leo, who didn't seem to mind. In fact, he was smiling.

"The box is for your *dad*?"

"Uh-huh," Leo answered, then he turned for the box and quietly moved through the water. "Be very quiet and careful; they're sensitive."

"Who are?" asked Remi.

"That smell of apple juice comes from only one flower, Remi. My mum never dreamed of trying to grow one, because it's the rarest flower in the world. But she told us about it: the ghost orchid."

"Cool," said Leo.

They both leaned over, staring into the white box, and there it was. The rarest flower of them all, in a full bloom of white.

"That's a cool-looking flower," said Remi. "And I don't even like flowers. You're right – it's like magic. And look – the box is made to hold it. It's got lights in the lid and on the floor. It's perfect."

The key card vibrated once more, and a final message appeared.

Six a.m. tomorrow, duck elevator.
Only Leo.

"It's okay," said Remi, seeing that Leo wished they could go together. "My mum and I don't get here until seven, anyway. Good luck, bro."

Leo shut the lid on the box and gently picked it up. When he did, a door popped open on the wall to the left of the field of flowers. There were white stairs leading down, which would take them back to the Flying Farm Room.

Where Ms Sparks awaited them both.

CHAPTER 14

FIRED!

Leo left Remi in the upper part of the hotel and crept down to the basement with the box. They both agreed that Remi would play the decoy, drawing Ms Sparks away if she appeared. The last person they wanted getting her hands on such a special box was old Beehive-head.

As Leo walked, the box dimmed slowly from light to dark. Night for the ghost orchid had come. Opening the door to the basement, Leo saw lights flashing against the walls.

"Oh no, more trouble," he said to himself. "At least the siren isn't going off."

As he crept down the stairs and peered around the

corner, he saw, to his relief, that his father wasn't there.

What was not so relieving was the state of the call centre. Daisy had spat out a rolling pile of twisted paper that looked like it was a mile long . . . and she was still going. The ticker tape of broken things in the hotel kept getting longer and longer, and all the lights on the call centre wall were flashing. Leo had never seen the call centre so wild with activity, so wild, in fact, that steam was pouring out of the corners of the wall. It looked as though the entire thing might explode at any moment.

But why no siren? Leo inspected the call centre more closely and saw that someone – probably his dad – had cut all the sound wires, which dangled and sparked against the wall.

"He must have grown tired of all the noise," Leo said, speaking this time to the ghost orchid hidden in the box. "Good thing. I know how loud noises bother you."

The ghost orchid was delicate. It bloomed over and over in the summer, but only if the conditions were right. Too much clatter or a storm – anything like that and the flower would close and might not ever open again.

"Better get you safely hidden away," said Leo, stepping over piles of ticker tape on the way to his bed.

As he slid the box under the bed, he took note of the four boxes that had gathered there: first the purple one, then the blue, then green, and now white. Four boxes.

He was arranging them just so when the door to the basement opened. He stood up, leaning against the washing machine as casually as he could. He expected to see his father, racing back for tools to fix this or that, but when he looked up, it was Ms Sparks. She had Remi by the ear, and he bounced down the stairs behind her, yelling for Leo to run.

"Shut up, pizza boy!"

Leo looked at the tiny window above his bed and wondered if he could reach it, climb through and run for the gate. He was *that* scared by the look on Ms Sparks's face.

"If you know what's good for you, you'll get to the Puzzle Room," she said. Leo could practically feel her icy cold breath. "NOW!"

Leo was terrified that the booming voice of Ms Sparks would kill the ghost orchid before he even had a chance to give it to his father. The thought sent him scurrying for the door, right past Ms Sparks as she slapped him on the back of the head.

Looking back, Leo saw that Ms Sparks was eyeing the basement, walking further into his home without being invited. She dragged Remi behind her and stood before the call centre.

"Are you coming?" asked Leo from the top of the stairs.

"I'll leave here when I please, and not a moment sooner," said Ms Sparks, looking at the boiler, the shelves of boxes, the washing machine. The beds.

"I'm going, then," said Leo, trying to distract her. "I'll be in the Puzzle Room, like you asked."

"Take your friend with you," said Ms Sparks, letting Remi go with a twist of her hand, as if she were snapping her fingers with his ear in between.

"Just so you know," said Remi, "that really hurt."

"GET OUT!" she screamed, and Leo's heart broke again. What rare and beautiful flower could possibly live in the same space as Ms Sparks's shrill voice?

Neither boy spoke as they walked through the lobby and into the Puzzle Room, having no idea what they might find there. All Leo could think about was Ms Sparks finding all four boxes, which would mean she'd know about the secret rooms. What then? What would she do? He was sure she was behind all the trouble at the hotel, sure it had been her at the gate with the black car, plotting the hotel's demise with a shady developer. She was driving down the price of the hotel and getting in on the deal. Or worse, she would *own* the Whippet with someone's help. It was a complete and total disaster in the making. Still, even those dark thoughts didn't prepare Leo for what awaited him in the Puzzle Room.

"You two are slow, slow, slow!" yelled Ms Sparks, who had crept up behind them and was now pushing them forwards.

"Sit down, there," she said, pointing to the only empty chairs in the room.

Leo's dad was sitting in the room, too, along with Remi's mum and Mr Phipps. It was the entire Whippet hotel staff: the hotel maid, the gardener and the maintenance man. And Ms Sparks, the hotel manager, was about to come unglued.

"I understand there was a party tonight," she began, clicking her fingernails on the long table that held the puzzle. "Which surprises me, since I wasn't invited. No one likes to be left out when there's a party, wouldn't you agree, *Mr Phipps?*"

She said it like an accusation, like she knew he hadn't attended the party.

"I don't know about any party," he said, calm and collected as he always was. "You had to wake me up for this meeting, remember?"

"Silence!" shouted Ms Sparks, her hand in his face. "Have you toured the grounds since I woke you? I suppose not. When you do, you'll find that someone has made a fool of you!"

"I don't know what you're talking about."

Ms Sparks knew how much Mr Phipps liked working on the puzzle, futile as it was, and how he especially liked to stack the pieces into groups that looked the same. She swept her hand across one of the neatly organized piles and sent puzzle pieces flying across the room.

"That's just mean," said Remi a little too loudly. Ms Sparks gave him the evil eye.

"I'll deal with you soon enough," she said, turning back to the gardener, who wouldn't look her in the eye.

"What you will find," Ms Sparks continued, "is that someone has taken shears to your beloved bushes."

"Why, that's impossible," said Mr Phipps, but he was clearly shaken. "I would have heard—"

"Ahhhh, you *would* have heard, if you weren't at a party."

"But I wasn't at the party!" said Mr Phipps. All he really wanted to do was get up and go and look at his garden, but Ms Sparks wasn't about to let him off that easily. Leo and Remi glanced at each other – Mr Phipps *hadn't* been at the party, or at least they hadn't seen him there.

"They've cut up all your sculpted bushes – the ducks, the rabbits – all of them."

"What?!" cried Mr Phipps. "But that's . . . well, it's . . ." He couldn't find the words to say. He'd spent years training the bushes and he loved the garden at the Whippet. It was probably the cruellest thing a person could do to a gardener.

Ms Sparks seemed satisfied to have tongue-tied Mr Phipps, so she moved on, pointing her long finger at Remi's mum.

"And you, responsible for keeping this place clean and tidy. What were you doing at a party when you're being paid to clean rooms?"

"I . . . well . . ." Pilar looked at Mr Fillmore, but there was nothing he could do. "I'd already cleaned all the rooms, and—"

"Save your excuses!" said Ms Sparks. "Maybe if you'd been attending to the hotel instead of dancing the night away, we wouldn't have a theft to deal with."

"A what?" asked Leo's dad, the first two words out of his mouth since they'd arrived in the room. There had never, ever been a theft of any kind in the five years he'd been the maintenance man. This was bad. *Very* bad. They always blamed the servants.

"A theft," Ms Sparks repeated, like she was talking to a room full of schoolchildren. "Someone has stolen Mrs Yancey's diamond necklace."

Pilar gasped, for she had seen the necklace in the Cake Room, lying unattended on a black velvet cloth in the bedroom. She'd been dusting the pink cupcake chairs and there it was.

"I see from your expression you know the necklace of which I speak," said Ms Sparks, leaning over the shaking Pilar. Remi couldn't help but notice the spider was gone, but oh, how he wished he had it back again. What he wouldn't give to drop it down Ms Sparks's trousers right now.

"That necklace," said Ms Sparks, "is worth more than all your salaries put together for the rest of your lives. She's convinced one of you took it. So am I."

"Well, of course she is," said Clarence Fillmore. "Who else is she going to blame?"

"Not that spoilt kid of theirs, that's for sure," said

Leo, which earned him an evil eye of his own from Ms Sparks.

"Quiet! All of you!" shouted Ms Sparks, turning her attention to Pilar. "I examined the contents of your trolley, and I think you know what I found."

Ms Sparks pulled the long diamond necklace slowly out of her pocket.

"I don't believe you," said Clarence Fillmore. "None of us do."

But Ms Sparks had already moved on, happy to have Clarence take centre stage as she put the necklace back in her pocket.

"And finally, you, Mr Fillmore; you with the tools and the belt and the overalls. You *look* like a maintenance man. What I don't understand is why you don't act like one."

"We can't help it if someone is sabotaging the hotel," said Leo. "Things are breaking faster than we can fix them, and you know it."

"All I know is that you were at a party, and while you were, the hotel fell into ruin. I couldn't find the maintenance crew, so I went searching. And do you know what I found?"

"Uh-oh," said Remi.

"Yes, uh-oh indeed, Remilio. I found *you*."

Ms Sparks pointed at both Leo and Remi.

"You were not at the party after all, were you?"

"We *were* at the party," Leo protested. "We just left for a minute."

"Oh, come now. You know that's not true. You were missing a long time. Long enough to cause all sorts of new problems, right? I mean, *really*, who would know better than you, Leo Fillmore, how to break things in this hotel?"

Leo and Remi and Mr Fillmore all protested, but Ms Sparks had the loudest voice of them all, and she silenced them. "Here's what I think. I think you're all in this together. I think it's all an elaborate setup. And do you know what else?"

Everyone sat silently, because they knew what was coming. She was the hotel manager. She could do it in Mr Whippet's absence if she chose to. If he ever returned, she would simply say they'd stolen from one of the guests. She had always known how to get what she wanted from Merganzer D Whippet.

"Here we go," Remi whispered to Leo. "Nice knowing you."

"You are all, each and every one of you," said Ms Sparks, drawing in a great breath of air and pausing for effect, "FIRED!"

Mr Phipps seemed not to care in the slightest, and the moment she said the word, he left the room to inspect the damage in the garden he'd put so much work into. He cared an awful lot about the Whippet. If he really were to leave, the grounds would never be the same.

Pilar looked at Leo's father, and Leo had the feeling that something might have bloomed, if only they'd had more time. He wasn't sure how he felt about the idea, but he wanted more than anything for his dad to be happy again. He'd been thinking that maybe the Fillmore men were finally ready to move on.

"Thanks for everything," Remi said, pulling Leo aside where they could talk one last time without being overheard. "It was the best day of my life, and I'm not just saying that. If you find Blop, say hello to him from me."

The two boys might as well have lived on different planets. Staten Island and Manhattan were worlds apart.

"I don't know what to say," Leo offered. "It feels like we were close to . . . *something*. We just can't work out what."

"You've got a date with destiny in the morning,

remember? Who knows, maybe our luck will change."

In all the chaos, Leo had totally forgotten: *Six a.m. tomorrow, duck elevator*. It wasn't much, but it was better than nothing.

Remi rejoined his mum, and Ms Sparks escorted them through the lobby and out of the front doors, where they stood staring through the glass. The doors were locked and the two started down the path for the underground station.

"I know you didn't take the necklace, Mum," said Remi.

"I know you do," said Pilar, putting an arm around him.

They walked in silence then, both of them dreaming of what might have been.

Ms Sparks was back in the Puzzle Room in no time flat with final instructions for the maintenance man and his son.

"Pack your things in the morning," she commanded. "I'll be bringing in a new crew by the afternoon. Enjoy your last night at the Whippet."

She patted her pocket and started for the stairs. "I've got some good news to deliver, wouldn't you say?"

And then, just like that, she was gone. Leo looked

around the room and suddenly realized something terrible. It wasn't just Ms Sparks who had left.

Everyone was gone.

Leo and his dad walked to the basement, maybe for the last time.

"We've really come to the end, I guess," said Clarence Fillmore. "I had hoped we'd see him again, but I think it's really true."

"What's true?"

Leo's big, lumbering father took a deep breath as he opened the door to the basement. "Merganzer D Whippet isn't coming back."

———

Bernard Frescobaldi was waiting in his black town car when Pilar and Remi unlocked the small pedestrian's gate and started down the wide, empty pavement. He noticed how unhappy they were, but made no effort to help them as they started their long night journey to Staten Island.

Milton smiled knowingly from the front seat.

"This is going better than I could have hoped," said Bernard, pulling his fedora down low over his eyes in case they searched the street. It wouldn't have mattered behind the dark windows, but Bernard was an exceptionally secretive man. He took no chances, especially when he was this close to the prize he'd worked so hard for.

Twenty minutes later, still sitting in the car, Bernard glanced at his very expensive watch.

"What's taking so long?" he asked. "I was sure the gate would open by now."

Five more minutes passed with Milton calming his wealthy boss, and then the vehicle gate opened up. Someone from the inside had opened it, letting the black town car in.

"Time to prepare for the meeting," said Bernard Frescobaldi. "Tomorrow, the Whippet Hotel will finally get the new owner it deserves."

The call centre in the basement had one giant plug, the head of which was bigger than a basketball with a ten-centimetre-wide cord to match. It took both Leo and his dad to pull it out of the wall, but when they did, Daisy stopped printing ticker tape. The shark, for the first time all day, was silent. All the lights on the wall went out, and for a split second, Leo imagined the Whippet Hotel as it once was: full of laughter and smiles, mystery and intrigue, not a care from the world outside.

Both Fillmore men got into their pyjamas and

brushed their teeth. They went about their business rather slowly, savouring every bitter-sweet moment in the cosy basement that had been their home for a good long time.

"Mum would have wanted a flower on a night like this," said Leo, risking the possibility of turning a very bad night into a sad one to boot. But he had a feeling, even with everything that had gone wrong, that something had changed. "Do you think about her?" Leo asked as they both lay down on their beds, the washing machine sitting quiet and cold between them.

Mr Fillmore stood up, looked about the room, then grabbed his camp bed by the edge and pulled the old frame out from the wall. He took hold of Leo's next, pulling that away from the wall as well, then he got back into bed and lay on his side, where he could see his boy's face.

"I should have done that years ago," said Leo's dad.

"Actually, the washing machine blocks your snoring, especially when it's running."

"Leo, listen to me now. We're going to be fine, and none of this is your fault."

Leo held back tears, because he was pretty sure it *was* his fault.

"And yes, I think about your mum all the time. I hope you do, too."

"I do, Dad."

There was a long silence in which Leo thought maybe a tear had fallen from his dad's eye, but it was dark and he couldn't be sure.

"I think she would have liked this place," Leo's dad said. "But more than that, I think she would have wanted us to keep living. You think?"

"I do, Dad."

Mr Fillmore held the ring on the chain, rubbing it as if it was a good luck charm. He'd had a hard time forgiving himself for letting it slip away during the move to the Whippet.

"I felt bad for losing your mother's ring. You know that, don't you?"

"Of course I know," Leo said. "It just happened, and anyway, it's back now."

Clarence Fillmore smiled. "It's different now. I still miss her, but I'm not so sad any more."

Leo leaned over and pulled the white box out from its hiding spot. He opened the lid and white light filled the room. The ghost orchid bloomed to life.

"I found this for us," said Leo. "I thought maybe

Ms Sparks had killed it, but I guess not."

The two of them couldn't help it then; maintenance men being notoriously emotional, they both shed a tear or two.

"Fresh start tomorrow?" asked Mr Fillmore, his voice filled with everything the moment demanded: sadness for what had been lost, unease about the future, but above all, something new – a readiness to start living again.

"Fresh start tomorrow," said Leo, sinking into his camp bed one last time.

They watched the ghost orchid for a time, and then Leo drifted off to sleep and Mr Fillmore closed the white box and silently carried it out of the basement.

He knew a certain gardener who needed a ghost orchid even more than he did.

· CHAPTER 15 ·

THE THIRTEENTH FLOOR

The alarm on Leo's watch went off at 5.30 in the morning, but it didn't matter. He had awoken with the first light of day to find the note stuck to his bedpost.

> *I THOUGHT MR PHIPPS COULD USE A LOOK*
> *AT THE GHOST ORCHID. HOPE YOU DON'T*
> *MIND. DAD*

The box was gone, and for a moment Leo worried he might need it for something. But barring that, he didn't plan to ask for the flower back. Mr Phipps would know how to care for it, and Leo's dad was right: it was the perfect gift for a displaced gardener who'd had his garden ransacked.

Leo turned off the alarm on his watch and adjusted his position in the duck elevator. He knew he had to be there at six, as the message had said, but there was no reason to wait. He might get sidetracked by some other duty or Ms Sparks might try to kick them out of the building on sight. Better to hide in the duck elevator and make sure he didn't miss the appointment altogether. It was an appointment, he was sure, that would not be offered twice.

At 5.47, Leo heard Ms Sparks come into the lobby and make some keys, for what, he did not know or care. A period of silence followed, and then, precisely at six o'clock, the duck elevator moved. Leo did not pull the lever or press the button for the roof, but either way, those things would never have made the elevator move as it did now. No, this was something new. The duck elevator was moving sideways, not up or down. It was, in fact, moving parallel to the lobby, under the grand staircase Leo had climbed many times.

The duck elevator stopped, and when it did, a section of the back wall slid slowly down, revealing four buttons and a frosted sheet of glass.

"Here we go," said Leo.

The finger was back, writing a message on the cold, frosted glass.

> *These buttons you only push once. Push them wrong at your own peril.*

Leo felt supremely excited as he read the message, because he knew then that his journey with Remi had given them the knowledge only they could possibly have. The only way a person could know the order in which to push purple, blue, green, and white buttons would be if they had four boxes to match. Leo had got the boxes in a certain order. He knew which button to push first, and so he did.

Purple.

The elevator moved abruptly sideways once more, this time in a different direction.

Leo pushed the next button.

Blue.

The elevator moved again, lurching to a stop.

Green was pushed and the elevator moved once more.

"Only one button left," said Leo. He wished Remi were with him, or at least Betty, Blop or Merle the flying goat. He felt suddenly very alone in the world as his finger hovered over the white button.

And then he pushed it.

The duck elevator began spinning in a circle, then it shot up through the Whippet Hotel as fast as the Double Helix had ever gone. Leo put his hands on the low ceiling and braced himself. Either the duck elevator was about to stop, or they were going right through the roof and into the air.

The duck elevator did stop, almost as suddenly as it had started.

The number 13 appeared above the four buttons with the sound of a bell.

"But there is no floor thirteen," Leo said. But even as he said it, he knew there had always been thirteen floors. He'd simply never been invited to any of the secret floors or the *very* secret floor at the top.

Leo took a deep breath to calm himself, threw open the duck elevator door and crawled out into the room.

He stood up, but did not speak. Overhead he saw the bottom of the pond, which he now realized was made of glass. He could see the duck feet flapping and the fish swimming. Light poured in through the pond, filling the thirteenth floor with a dreamy, golden hue. There were books every where, on tables and endless shelves winding this way and that. There were long, lazy-looking couches and overstuffed chairs. There were huge beanbags, some pink like a pig and others black-and-white like dairy cows. Coloured rings of every size drifted near the ceiling, held by some unknowable magnetic force, and flying holographic farm animals swooped high and low. But mostly there were books. Lots and lots of books.

"It's the library," Leo found himself saying, for it was indeed the Whippet Library, where Merganzer came to think, think and think some more.

A perfectly silent train made its way around the wide perimeter. There was someone on the train, and Leo knew him right away. He was dressed in black, which was not his normal attire, but it was him, there could be no doubt.

"Welcome to the thirteenth floor," said the man. "I hope you like it as much as I do."

"Mr Phipps?" asked Leo, because it was none other than the gardener himself.

"Thank you for the ghost orchid. I was hoping you might let me have it."

"You're welcome," said Leo, because he couldn't think of anything else to say.

"And now I have something rather important to give you, something that was left in my care."

Leo was so confused and amazed, he just stood in the library, gawking at the gardener, unable to speak.

Mr Phipps took a leather case out of his black jacket and unzipped it. From inside he pulled a silver chain, and on the end of the silver chain sat the Whippet Hotel's sole silver key card.

"Is that . . . ?" Leo began, but he couldn't finish.

"Merganzer D Whippet's silver key card? The one that unlocks every door, even the many hidden doors? Yes, it is."

"Why do you have it?" asked Leo.

Mr Phipps took a piece of folded paper from the same leather case and held it with the key card in one hand.

"You love the Whippet Hotel, don't you, Leo?"

"Of course I do."

"Then take the silver key card."

Leo reached out his hand, not really sure what it meant to have the key, and then took the paper with it.

"Put the silver key card around your neck and the paper in your pocket," Mr Phipps instructed.

Leo hung the chain around his neck and put the

paper in the front pocket of his maintenance overalls.

"What's the paper?" he asked.

"Why, it's the deed to the Whippet Hotel, of course. Why else would you have the silver key card?"

"The *what*?"

Mr Phipps looked Leo in the eye and smiled. "Leo Fillmore, you own the Whippet Hotel. At least for the moment."

Leo felt as if he might stop breathing. Could it really be true? No, it could not. Something wasn't right.

"Who gave you the authority to give *me* the Whippet Hotel? Only Merganzer can do that, and he's missing."

He hated to say the next part, because he really liked Mr Phipps.

"Did you steal the silver key card from Mr Whippet?"

Mr Phipps was a patient man, but there were things to be done and little time to do them in.

"Climb aboard – we've got to go somewhere."

Leo didn't know if he could trust Mr Phipps, but there seemed to be some plan in motion, and he certainly didn't know of any other way out of the Whippet Library. Stepping into the train carriage and sitting down, he asked the gardener another question.

"So you're the mysterious Mr M? It's you who's been following me and Remi around all this time, scaring us half to death with that finger of yours."

"*Helping* you. And keeping Captain Rickenbacker entertained, which is no easy task, let me tell you."

"But why?"

Mr Phipps wouldn't answer as the train followed a track that wound higher and higher until he had to duck in order to miss the ceiling. Or did he? Was the ceiling a hologram, too? It would appear so, because they went right through it and came to a hidden station on the other side.

"You'll have to get out of the train now," said Mr Phipps.

Leo stepped out on to a lonely platform, where a set of stairs led up into darkness.

"Up there, you'll find your way," said Mr Phipps. "He's a crafty one, so be careful what you say. Good luck."

The train pulled away, disappearing down into the Whippet Library, and Leo was alone.

"I wish Remi were here," he said, climbing the stairs until his hand bumped up against the ceiling. He pushed and light poured in. If Leo could have seen the world from the other side, he would have watched as a square of grass on the roof opened up and a boy peeked out.

"Over here, and make it snappy. You don't want to keep Mr Frescobaldi waiting."

"Mr who?" asked Leo, stepping out on to the roof and letting the trapdoor slam shut behind him. There was a short man standing before him whom he had never seen before.

"Come, come," said the man, waving Leo on. "This way. He's waiting for you."

Leo saw the ducks in the pond, though Betty wasn't there. He thought about whistling three times fast and calling her, but what good would having a duck by his side do?

"I'm not going anywhere until you tell me who you are," said Leo.

The man hesitated and seemed poised to tell a lie.

"My name is Milton. Satisfied? Now please, come quickly. This will all be over before you know it."

There had always been a small stand of trees on the roof in the far corner, away from the pond. In amongst the trees was a stone bench, and on the bench sat Bernard Frescobaldi. He had on a long grey coat with the collar turned up, black glasses and a black fedora. He was staring out over the city.

"Who are you and how did you get up here?" asked Leo. Leo didn't know who these people were, but he didn't like the idea of two total strangers on the roof of the Whippet. The man in the long grey coat would not turn around, but he signalled with his hand, and Milton came near. Leo watched as they whispered, then Milton delivered the message.

"We understand that you have the silver key card and the deed to the hotel, and we have an offer for you."

Leo was on red alert, and thought seriously about calling Betty or running for the trapdoor. Mr Phipps was a traitor, probably in on the deal with Ms Sparks and whoever these two were.

"You give us the silver key card and the deed," continued Milton. He coughed, as if the next thing he was about to say was going to hurt. "And we will give you fifty million dollars."

Leo's jaw dropped. Fifty *million* dollars? He had no idea how much the Whippet was worth, but fifty million would mean . . . a lot. His dad would never have to work again. He could buy Remi and Pilar a real house. He could go to college. Still, if the Whippet really was his, didn't he have an obligation to protect it from a wrecking ball and, more importantly, from that awful Ms Sparks?

Leo watched as the man in the long grey coat whispered to Milton once more.

"It's falling apart, anyway," Milton went on. "And you don't know how to run a hotel. We'll offer fifty million, not a penny more."

Little did Leo know that the land the Whippet sat on, not to mention the countless treasures inside, was worth at least ten times that. But the truth was, it didn't matter. No amount of money was going to get Leo to give up the Whippet Hotel. He'd already made up his mind. He belonged here. He wanted to stay.

"You're standing on the roof of my hotel, and I want you off," he said. "Both of you. I love this place, and you can't have it."

Milton looked stunned as the man in the long grey coat stood up abruptly. He still would not turn around, and Leo had just about had it with whoever this guy was. He whistled three times fast, hoping to get some help from a duck, and then Milton started smiling.

"I told you this would happen. I told you!"

Leo whistled three times again, and this time he

heard Betty quacking, but she would not come.

"If you did anything to my duck, you're in big trouble," said Leo.

"Betty is busy," said the man in the long grey coat.

"What did you say?" Leo asked, not because he hadn't heard, but because he had. He knew that voice.

"She's laid her eggs and is going to have babies!" yelled the man in the long grey coat, and he threw off his hat, which revealed a wild whip of hair that simply would not stay down no matter how hard he tried. He turned – and it was not Bernard Frescobaldi, for there was no Bernard Frescobaldi. It was Merganzer D Whippet, as it always had been.

"Merganzer?" Leo gasped, first smiling, then laughing and running and hugging his old friend.

"The one and only! Me, me and only me! And did you hear the news? Betty's having BABIES!"

It was just like Merganzer to be excited about a duck, but Leo had to admit, the timing couldn't have been better. There had been a lot of talk about mothers lately.

Merganzer grabbed Leo by the hand and hauled him down the path of trees, then sat down, clapping his hands. "You see there, she's built her nest."

No wonder Betty had been so cranky all week, Leo thought.

"Six eggs," said George Powell, for Milton wasn't Milton, either; he was George, Merganzer's oldest and dearest friend.

"Leo, meet George. We've got a lot to talk about."

"It would seem so," said Leo, who still didn't believe any of it.

Merganzer talked and talked, as Merganzer was known to do, so it was hard to get a word in edgewise. But Leo tried his best.

"First of all," Merganzer said, "you passed. You passed, you passed, you passed! I had my doubts, really

I did. Ask George; he'll tell you. I thought you might give up. But you took everything I threw at you and kept on going. Even that last part, which I simply had to do. You passed that one, too."

Leo didn't quite understand, so George tried to explain.

"I've always stayed away from the hotel, which was by design, because Merganzer knew this day might come, a day when he would have to leave the Whippet and move on to other, more pressing matters. I must say I had my doubts as well, but now that I've seen you in action, my doubts have completely vanished. It was one thing to find all the boxes and overcome so very much; we thought you had that in you. But to say no to so much money, when you really could have used it! Well, that was the most important thing. That was why we had to do things the way we did."

"But I still don't understand," said Leo, turning back to Merganzer. "You can't mean it. You can't really want to give me the Whippet Hotel."

"Oh, but you're wrong, Leo," Merganzer replied. "I *do* want to give you the hotel. I *can't* keep it; too much to do, too many places to go. You're the only one for the Whippet."

"But what about Mr Phipps or my dad or Ms Sparks?"

Even Leo couldn't believe he'd said her name, but she *was* the hotel manager, and she *had* pulled the wool over Merganzer's eyes for a long time.

"Leo, listen to me," said Merganzer. "It's you, you're the one. No one else will do. Don't you see?"

But Leo didn't see. He simply couldn't do it.

Merganzer took a long silver pen from his coat pocket and held out his hand for the deed to the Whippet Hotel. Leo gave it back to him.

"We have a lot in common, us two," said Merganzer. "We both lost our mums too soon. We both want to remember. But there comes a day when we have to move on."

Merganzer D Whippet signed the deed over to Leo and handed the paper back, winking at George as he did.

"And we both found that a true friend can help carry us through lonely times. Am I right, George?"

"So right, so true."

"Remi," Leo said, thinking of his new friend and wondering what he must be going through. His mum didn't have a job and his dad had gone missing. They might not even be able to pay the rent.

"You have the silver key card now, Leo, and that means you can open any door. Not just the doors in this hotel, but all the doors you're going to find for the rest of your life."

Leo held the silver key card in his hand.

"Will you be here to help me?" he asked. "It's an awful lot to look after."

"You'll see me, once in a while. And George, too. Don't forget – you've got lots of help if you know where to look."

Leo had some thoughts about that, and suddenly

he couldn't wait to get cracking on all the problems plaguing the hotel.

"There's a lot to fix around here," said Leo.

"Speaking of which, we have some business to attend to."

Merganzer got to his feet and pulled a whistle out of his pocket, blowing it twice.

"What sort of business?" asked Leo, running up behind him.

"House-cleaning."

Leo felt a tingle in his toes at the idea of what Merganzer D Whippet might be talking about.

· CHAPTER 16 ·

ALL IS REVEALED

If there was one thing Leo could say for sure about Merganzer D Whippet, it was this: the guy knew how to make an entrance. It began all the way up on the seventh floor, where he donned his hat and glasses. He knocked on all the guests' doors, and each time he turned away and flipped the collar up on the coat so that his face could not be seen.

"Is it time already?" one of the guests said. "I trust everything went as planned?"

"Yes, everything, exactly as we planned it," said George, whom the guest knew only as Milton, Bernard Frescobaldi's driver. "Meet us in the lobby, won't you?"

"I look forward to concluding our business, Mr Frescobaldi," said the guest, but Bernard was already gone, down the stairs until he had summoned every single guest to the lobby. He had sent Leo ahead to find his father, and the two maintenance men waited at the bottom of the wide staircase as Merganzer D Whippet, fully disguised as Bernard Frescobaldi, strode down the steps.

Ms Sparks saw him first.

"Who on earth is *that*?" she said, one eye on the mysterious man in the long grey coat and one on the front door. She seemed to be pondering whether or not to run, though it was hard to say why. There was something about this man she recognized.

Merganzer reached the bottom of the stairs as the guests started arriving, some by the main elevator, some by the stairs, all of them curious.

"I'll have you know that mornings are my best writing hours," said Theodore Bump. "You may have just cost me five thousand words. This had better be important."

Captain Rickenbacker was not a morning person, and he arrived with his red cape tucked into his trousers. "Has anyone made coffee?" was all he said.

The Yanceys huddled together in their matching

black silk pyjamas, completely confused.

LillyAnn Pompadore set Hiney on the floor, where he promptly peed.

"Pilar!" Ms Sparks yelled, and it was only after she heard her own voice that she remembered she'd fired the maid the night before. She looked around the room and her eyes landed on Leo. "You, clean that up."

"Yes, ma'am," said Leo, who always carried a can of carpet-cleaning foam and rags in his tool bag, just in case.

"Is someone going to tell us why we're here?" asked Mr Yancey. "If not, I believe I'll go back to my room. I'd like to make sure nothing gets stolen."

It was a jab Leo didn't like to hear, especially from a paying customer at the hotel he now owned.

Merganzer had remained quiet, seated in the darkest corner of the lobby, but now he snapped his fingers. His best friend in all the world came down the stairs.

"George Powell?" said Ms Sparks. "What are you doing here?"

Ms Sparks was alarmed, because Mr Powell *never* came to the hotel. She'd only ever seen him in his private legal office seven streets away, and even then very rarely.

"Who's George Powell? You mean him?" asked LillyAnn Pompadore, pointing at the short man arriving

at the bottom of the stairs. "That's Milton, not George."

Ms Sparks smelled a rat, looking at the door once more, and came out from behind the check-in counter.

"What's the meaning of this, George?" Ms Sparks demanded.

"I believe I'll let him tell you," George said, pointing to Merganzer. When he did, Merganzer threw off the disguise and everyone gasped, for they all knew who it was in an instant.

"My apologies for gathering you all so early, but I'm afraid it was unavoidable," Merganzer began without the slightest hesitation. Ms Sparks was utterly speechless as George Powell unlocked the hotel door and Mr Phipps came in, back to looking every bit the gardener.

"I'm only here for a moment and then I must go, this time for good," said Merganzer. "Just a few loose ends to tie up, then I'm off."

"But you're not Mr Whippet," said LillyAnn Pompadore. "You're Bernard Frescobaldi. And he's Milton, your driver."

"I'm afraid not," said Merganzer, looking at all the long-term guests. He walked over to Theodore Bump, who had been with the hotel for two years running. As Bernard Frescobaldi, Merganzer had called Mr Bump on several occasions, offering money for causing chaos at the hotel. Each time, Theodore Bump had refused.

"Keep writing those books," said Merganzer. "I'm a very fast reader, you know. I do hope you'll stay on after I'm gone."

"Keep Blop out of my room, and you've got a deal."

Merganzer glanced at Leo, who nodded.

"Done," said Mr Whippet.

Leo had finished cleaning up after Hiney by then, and stood next to his dad, wondering where this was going.

"And you," said Merganzer, stopping in front of Captain Rickenbacker. "What will the Whippet do if you don't protect us from Mr M, hmmm?"

Bernard had called Captain Rickenbacker to the gate on two occasions, asking for dastardly favours, but Captain Rickenbacker had never wavered.

"You can count on me," said Captain Rickenbacker, saluting Merganzer enthusiastically.

Merganzer bent down and picked up Hiney.

LillyAnn Pompadore had been inching her way towards the door, but when Merganzer picked up her dog, she stopped.

"Give me my dog and I'll be on my way," she said.

"Ms Pompadore, you were all too willing."

"My husband has a lot of money, more than you, I'm sure!" she fired back. "He might just buy this hotel right out from under you!"

Merganzer handed Ms Pompadore her dog. She held him close and looked as if she might start crying.

"Then why did you do it, Ms Pompadore? Why did you agree to sabotage the hotel?"

"Because you said – *Bernard* said – it would drive down the price. You said we could own it together!"

"But LillyAnn," said Merganzer, far too kindly for someone who had totally betrayed him, "you just said you could buy it out from under me."

"No, that's not true. I said *my husband* could buy it," said LillyAnn, and then she began to cry, holding Hiney close to her chest. "My *ex-husband*, if you want the truth."

But Merganzer already knew about that. It was why he knew LillyAnn might betray him, but he also knew the *real* reason why, and this softened his heart.

"Where will I go?" asked LillyAnn. "The Whippet

is the only home I've got, and I'm all out of money. It's just me and Hiney now."

"You love the Whippet, don't you, LillyAnn?" asked Merganzer.

"I do, and I'm sorry. I'm very, very sorry."

Captain Rickenbacker put an arm around LillyAnn and patted her gently. He petted the dog, because the two of them were close friends.

"I could use Hiney," said Captain Rickenbacker. "He's a good sniffer."

"And I see a marvellous story here," said Theodore Bump. "It could be my biggest seller yet, but I'll need to interview the young lady."

LillyAnn Pompadore brightened at the sound of the word *young* and stepped a little closer to Mr Bump. She looked at Merganzer as if he held her whole life on a delicate string.

Merganzer glanced once more at Leo, who nodded very slightly.

"Of course you can stay," said Merganzer D Whippet. "But you'll have to do some work around here. No one gets by for free."

LillyAnn beamed, but it was the last straw for Ms Sparks, who had watched the proceedings with increasing discomfort.

"You must evict her, Mr Whippet. She can't be trusted!" she yelled. "None of this lot can be trusted! This hotel has become a den of liars, scoundrels and reckless, rude children. I will not stand for it!"

Merganzer was a gentle soul, but every now and then, when duty called, he could be a lion. He walked up to Ms Sparks, looking down his long, elegant nose as she leaned away from him. He stood so close, the beehive pointed towards the wall behind her.

And then he spoke.

"I don't want to alarm the guests, but you, Ms Sparks, are fired."

"You can't fire me! I'm the hotel manager!" she shouted. Merganzer snuck his hand into her jacket pocket and pulled the long diamond necklace out slowly.

"My necklace!" said Nancy Yancey, snatching it away from Merganzer almost before he could get it all the way out into the open.

Everyone gasped at once, even Mr Phipps, who was nearly unflappable.

"Mr Fillmore, would you please escort Ms Sparks out of the hotel," asked Merganzer. Clarence Fillmore was the biggest man in the room by miles, and before Ms Sparks knew it, he was standing at her side.

"You can't fire me! You can't!" cried Ms Sparks.

"Actually, you're right about that," said Merganzer. "I can't fire you."

Ms Sparks looked momentarily triumphant, holding her head high. She might prevail over this weakling after all.

"Leo, have you the key card and the deed?" asked Merganzer.

Leo came to the middle of the room and pulled out the rarest of the Whippet key cards – and Ms Sparks nearly fell over backwards. Mr Fillmore knew about the card, too. They all did, and none of them could believe Leo was holding it.

"But how—?" Ms Sparks stammered.

"You are all witnesses here, each and every one of you," said Merganzer D Whippet. "I hereby sell the Whippet Hotel and everything in it to Leo Fillmore for the price of –" He glanced back and forth around the room until he saw the thing Leo held in his hand. "I sell the Whippet Hotel and everything in it to Leo Fillmore for the price of one bottle of carpet cleaner!"

It was all theatrics, but Leo handed Merganzer the bottle of carpet cleaner, which was then handed to George Powell for safe keeping. Leo held up the deed for everyone to see, and then he looked up at Ms Sparks.

"You're fired," he said.

Ms Sparks started taking things off the check-in desk, anything she could put her hands on – the appointment book, the pens, pads of paper. Mr Fillmore took them all back, one by one, and ushered her to the door. Leo smiled from ear to ear. Could it get any better? He didn't think so as Ms Sparks screamed on her way out.

"This won't be the last you see of me, Leo Fillmore!"

Merganzer D Whippet looked at George. "How did I ever manage to hire that woman to begin with?"

"You see the best in people," said George. "But I'll admit, you have to look awfully hard to find anything good in that one. She can be quite deceptive."

Merganzer leaned in close to Leo and gave him a piece of advice.

"Know thy enemy."

Leo nodded, because he understood. Ms Sparks would do almost anything to win back control of the Whippet. Maybe it wasn't really the last time he would see her.

A stillness invaded the lobby, and Merganzer

ushered everyone into the Puzzle Room, where he had one more surprise before his departure.

"This one is for you, Mr Phipps. And you, Captain Rickenbacker."

He took a black key card out of his pocket, swiped the surface back and forth and back again with his elegantly long finger, and the puzzle pieces began rising into the air. All eight hundred thousand of them. It was like a puzzle snowstorm over the long table, and everyone laughed.

"How?" asked Mr Phipps.

"I could tell you how each piece has its own magnet," said Merganzer. "And I could tell you about the complex system of magnets in the table and throughout the room. But let's just say it's a bit of magic, shall we?"

"Works for me," said Captain Rickenbacker.

Merganzer swiped the black key card again and pieces started to fall into place. The room filled with the sound of snapping as thousands of puzzle pieces locked into place. Leo thought it was the most spectacular thing he'd ever seen.

When it was done, there were indeed two hundred and twenty-three ducks, including Betty and the other resident ducks, all six of them waddling towards a bright green pond. There were trees and a blue sky, the grounds with their giant topiaries, and the Whippet Hotel right in the middle of it all.

"Not bad," said Leo. "Not bad at all."

It had been the most magical of mornings, but Leo still had a certain emptiness inside that he could not shake. He tapped George on the shoulder, hoping for one last favour.

"I wonder if you might play the part of Milton one last time," asked Leo. "There's someone I need to go find."

"I was hoping you might ask," said George. He donned his driving cap and bowed to the new owner of the Whippet Hotel. "After you, sir."

And they were off.

· CHAPTER 17 ·

GOODBYE, FOR NOW

Leo stood in front of a door that reminded him of how thankful he was to be living at the Whippet Hotel. The building in which the door found its home was not cared for the way a building should be. Leo had spied hundreds of things he would have liked to fix on the way up, and he was sure there were thousands more.

"If I owned this building, it would be in much better shape," said Leo.

"That's the spirit," said George. "Maybe you *will* own it one day."

Leo looked across at his companion and wondered how that would be possible.

"Better knock; time's a-wasting," George encouraged. And so Leo did knock, softly at first, and then louder because he was so excited.

When Pilar saw him, her eyes brightened.

"Leo! How did you –?" She seemed to let the question go as it trailed off, suddenly happy for her son. "Remilio is going to be so happy to see you. The hotel is all he talks about."

Pilar let them in and Leo's heart sank a little. She had done her best to fix up the one-bedroom flat, but there was only so much a mum could do with cracked windows, ancient appliances and holes in the walls.

"You've really fixed it up nicely," said George, holding out his hand. "I'm George Powell. I work for Mr Whippet."

"Oh," said Pilar, not sure what to make of the small man before her. "Are you here about the necklace?"

"No, no, no," said George, feeling terrible for having worried her so. "That mystery has been solved, and it has nothing to do with you. We came for a different reason."

Remi was in the postage-stamp-size kitchen, slurping down a bowl of cereal, when they came around the corner.

"Hi, Remi," said Leo. Remi was so excited to hear Leo's voice, he whipped around in his seat and knocked the cereal bowl over. But he didn't care. None of them did, because Leo didn't waste any time spilling the good news. He told them about Merganzer's return, Ms Pompadore, and Ms Sparks.

"I knew she set us up!" said Remi, so excited that he hugged his mother right there in front of everyone. When Leo told them he'd inherited the Whippet Hotel, Remi flipped on an old kitchen radio set to a Spanish station, got up on the kitchen table and started dancing.

"He does that sometimes," said Pilar, equally excited but less showy.

"Why am I not surprised?" asked Leo, and then he asked Pilar a very important question.

"Pilar, will you please come and work for me?" He was hiring his first employee, and it felt good. "And live at the Whippet Hotel, too? You can have Ms Sparks's old room."

Pilar started to breathe strangely.

"Stand back," said Remi, still dancing, only even more excitedly now. "She's going to lose it!"

Pilar started to cry, then she started to dance, her hands over her head. Pretty soon they were all dancing, even George Powell, who was not known for letting his emotions run away with him.

In the end, they decided to leave everything behind, get in the black town car and depart the old flat without looking back. Leo promised to send a removal company to get each and every last thing so they could decorate Ms Sparks's old room and make it their own.

Pilar sat in the front seat with George, talking about her plans to make the maid service more efficient. George was immediately impressed with Leo's first new appointment.

Leo and Remi were in the back seat, whispering to each other.

"Is there a thirteenth floor, like I thought?" asked Remi.

"There is. I'll show it to you."

"So that's where you'll stay, then, you and your dad, on thirteen?"

Leo had thought a lot about this. "No, it's not that kind of room. It's all the secret rooms at once, and a library, too."

"You like libraries," said Remi. "I'm happy for you. But where will you stay?"

"We maintenance men like it in the basement,

where we can see all the action," said Leo, and it was true. For Leo, the basement was the heart of the Whippet. It was where he and his dad belonged.

"Thanks, Leo. For everything. You're the best friend I've ever had."

Leo pulled out the silver key card and showed it to Remi.

"Ditto everything you just said, times ten."

———

Merganzer was making his final tour through the ground floor of the hotel when he met Remi for the first time. He took a good look at the boy, tapping him once on each shoulder and declared him the Whippet Hotel's temporary doorman, until school started again in September.

"You'll need someone to help you pass the time," said Merganzer. "I know how boring it can get now and then."

Merganzer had changed into a more appropriate iridescent green jacket that was two sizes too large. He put his hand inside one of the great pockets, scrabbling around as many objects clanged together, and pulled out a little robot.

"This should do," said Merganzer, holding it out to Remi.

"Blop! I thought I'd never see you again!"

"Take good care of him for me, won't you?" asked Merganzer, a wisp of a tear in his eye. He was getting near the end, and it was proving harder than he'd thought it would be to say goodbye.

"Of course I will. And I'll take care of Leo, too. Don't you worry about a thing."

That was it, then, the tears were falling, and Merganzer turned for the Double Helix and one last meeting with the new owner of his hotel. Leo was waiting for him there, as he expected, holding the small orange door open.

"One last time, just for fun?" asked Leo.

"One last time, just for fun."

Two people never laughed and screamed so loudly as Leo and Merganzer D Whippet on the way up to the roof. The journey was too short, of course, but neither of them would forget it. The ride was always best when it was the two of them together.

"I think Betty will need to stay with the eggs," said Merganzer as they peeked around the tree and saw her nesting. "Shall we take the others on their walk?"

"Yes, sir," said Leo. "And don't you worry about a thing. Betty is very responsible. She'll be a good mum."

"I believe you're right," said Merganzer, but it was

still hard for him to leave without seeing the duck-lings hatch.

Mr Whippet smiled at Leo, thinking once again what a good choice he'd made. They hailed the duck elevator and shooed all the ducks but Betty inside, then crammed in with them. It was a very tight fit, especially for Merganzer, whose knees touched the ceiling of the elevator. All the ducks stared up at Merganzer inquisitively.

"My, but I love a good duck. They will be missed."

"If you keep talking like that, I'm going to think you're never coming back," said Leo. If he was hoping for some reassurance, he got none.

"I like Remi and his mum. George does, too," said Merganzer. "Take good care of them, will you?"

"Of course I will."

When they reached the lobby, Merganzer took his walking stick and hat and ushered the ducks out of the elevator. They waddled in a perfect line past Remi and Blop, and the robot began talking about webbed feet and ducks' bills.

"I'm going to miss our conversations," Merganzer said as he passed by, and Blop turned at the sound of his voice, as if somehow he knew it would be the last time he'd hear it.

Into the garden they went: the ducks, Mr Whippet, and Leo Fillmore. Merganzer took the black card out of his pocket, the one that had sent puzzle pieces flying.

"If you want to reset the puzzle, click here, here and then here. It's double-sided."

"You mean there are two sides to the puzzle?"

"Oh yes, of course there are. It's quite a secret, the other side. I suggest you don't see it for a while. You'll know when the time is right."

They made a wide loop on the soft trails, drinking in the rolling hills of green grass. When they came to the pond, they saw Leo's dad and Pilar, talking quietly.

"I wonder where that will go, and how you will feel about it," asked Merganzer.

"I don't know and I don't know," said Leo, "but I think it's going to be okay."

"You're right; it's unwise to meddle in such things. Let nature take its course and all that."

"By the way," said Leo, thinking back on the adventure he'd had. "Where did you find my mother's ring?"

Merganzer laughed quietly. "You remember last year, the trip you took?"

How could Leo forget? Yankees versus Red Sox, one of the great baseball matches at Fenway Park.

"Your father wouldn't take an extra penny unless he worked for it, but those Fenway tickets —" Merganzer whistled through his teeth. "Expensive. And the train, the hotel, the hot dogs —"

"He sold you the ring?"

"Oh no, not sold. Just collateral. There was no use trying to talk him out of it."

Leo remembered the extra Saturdays his dad had been working ever since, all so they could take some time off and watch baseball together.

They walked further still, towards the great black gate, and passed by Mr Phipps, trimming the green bushes into new and interesting shapes.

"Could I request an elephant sometime?" asked Leo. "Remi likes them."

"Consider it done," said Mr Phipps. He smiled, the old black freckles on his dark skin crumpling up against his eyes. "And you, sir, what will it be?"

Merganzer gazed over the grounds and found, at least for today, that it was just as it should be.

"I think that one, there on the end, would make a good elephant. When the time is right."

"As you wish, Mr Whippet."

"Keep Captain Rickenbacker occupied, will you?"

Mr Phipps held up his finger and wrote a tick in the air, smiling wistfully.

Somehow, without Leo really paying attention to how it had happened, they arrived at the gate to the hotel. It opened, slowly, and the black town car pulled up. George Powell rolled down the window.

"It's time for us to go," he said, as if they were late for something they'd been waiting all their lives to do.

Merganzer D Whippet took in a deep breath and looked back at his hotel. Then he handed Leo the walking stick and took off his iridescent green jacket.

"It's ten sizes too big," said Leo, swimming in the jacket as Merganzer draped it over his small shoulders.

"I have a good feeling you'll grow into it."

The ducks started to wander off towards the hotel, and Leo tapped the walking stick on the path.

When he turned back to the gate, the car was pulling away.

"If you need me," Merganzer yelled from the back seat, "search the field of wacky inventions!"

The car pulled away and the gate closed. Leo scratched his head, because he had no idea where the field of wacky inventions was. But he felt better, knowing he could search for his old friend if he needed him, which he was sure he would. He was ten and he owned a hotel. Not just any hotel, the Whippet, the strangest hotel in the world.

There would be challenges, lots of them.

Things would break.

Ms Sparks might try to come back.

Someone else would probably try to buy the hotel in order to build a skyscraper on the land.

But Leo had his dad and a peaceful memory of his mother. There would be Pilar and Mr Phipps, Captain Rickenbacker, Theodore Bump, LillyAnn Pompadore, and Betty. And there would be Remi. Leo wouldn't be doing this alone. He'd have plenty of help.

Looking up at the Whippet Hotel, he decided what he would do first.

He would take his dad, Pilar, Mr Phipps and Remi to the roof. And there, in the light of the morning sun, they would wave goodbye to Merganzer D Whippet.

A duck quacked in the distance and Leo ran, the Whippet Hotel rising to meet him, larger and closer, as Merganzer's green jacket trailed on the grass.

⸻

"Do you think he'll be all right?" asked Merganzer.

He, too, was looking at the Whippet Hotel. It was getting smaller and smaller as they went.

"I do," said George. "I do indeed."

"Maybe I should have mentioned the other floors."

"I think he probably knows enough for now."

Merganzer nodded and a wide smile filled his face. "He's a good boy."

"They both are," George agreed.

The Whippet Hotel was almost out of sight, and Merganzer began to feel free. He put his head out of the window and let his wild hair blow in the wind.

"A good day to be outside with the rabbits," he yelled.

"Indeed it is," said George.

They drove on, out of the city.

And the Whippet Hotel disappeared from view.